THE FALLEN GATES

GATES

The Oracle's Odyssey

Book 2

S. T. Hobbs

Book and Cover design by germancreative

Map design by BMR Williams
ISBN: 979-8-9857217-7-5
First Edition: July 2023
10 9 8 7 6 5 4 3 2 1

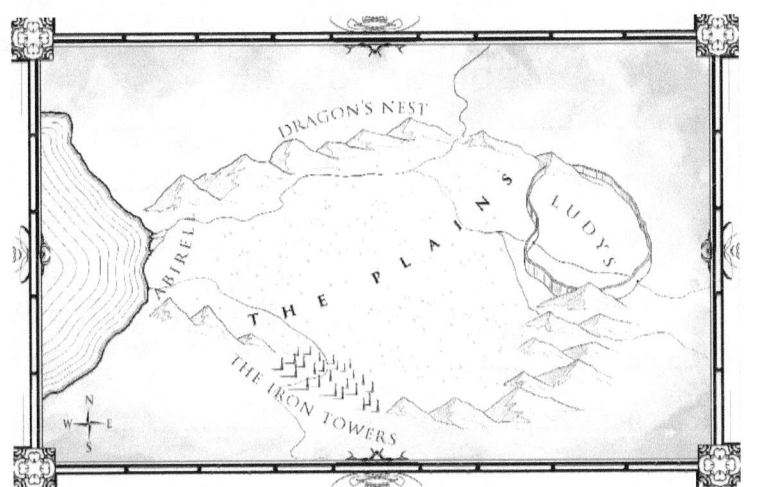

Table of Contents

PROLOGUE

IN THE LIBRARY OF THE IRON Towers, the *Chronicles of Fentra* lies buried beneath a layer of dust and cobwebs. It tells of the day the last oracle was killed and of the high council that met and decided her death. It tells of the day the world broke and humanity lost their way. It tells of the curse laid upon time that day. It tells of how the high king fell that day and the world was split; the four gateways no longer united under the banner of the high king; the men of the high council driven out to forever wander the plains with their kin and households.

It tells of the Silence that followed when the Fates retreated from the world and neither appeared nor spoke to any one.

All of this the *Chronicles of Fentra* tells to any who is able and willing to read it.

But the *Chronicles of Fentra* lies unread and forgotten, a piece of history lost to time and memory. A piece of history meant to shape the future.

For time is a circle. What has happened before will happen again and what will happen has already happened. On and on it shall go until the ending of days when time shall begin again.

CHAPTER 1

YOU ARE FENTRA'S CURSE."

Rensi's words dragged me out of a troubled dream and into a troubled reality. Wind whistled across the empty plains, tugging at me as I sat up and bringing with it a hint of spring warmth. In the weeks that had passed since I'd left her in the mountains, Rensi's final words to me had dug their way deep into my consciousness. Every time I tried to forget them, they clawed their way in deeper.

They were cruel words coming from her. Cruel words accompanied by cruel accusations. She blamed me for what had happened to her family. She blamed me for the fall of Dragon's Nest. Probably, she blamed me for what was coming to Abirell.

I tried to shake off those accusations the same as I did her cryptic words, but neither left me alone.

Because she was right.

At least, she was mostly right.

I could have warned Drakkus. I could have told him of the coming attack rather than just let it happen and let him die. But he could have taken the tether off, he could have let me return to my family and warn them. I'd only done to him what he'd done to me.

The only difference was that I survived, and he didn't.

She was completely right, though, about Dragon's Nest and Abirell. I saw the fall of both of them often in my dreams. Dragon's Nest erupting in a burst of brilliant orange, bathing the night sky in its fiery glow.

It was Abirell, silent and still, with death stalking her streets in the form of the plague that haunted me the most, though. The sorrow that had first accompanied the vision I'd had of Abirell's fall clung to every dream I'd had of it since. It made waking a mercy, even if I was waking alone with nothing but the wind to keep me company.

Long weeks I'd spent alone, each step drawing me closer to the south, to the Iron Towers where I'd find my family.

It was no easy thing.

The plains were not meant to be survived alone. Had it not been for the abundance of newly born animals that were easy to hunt along the way, I would likely have never made it anywhere near the Iron Towers.

"You are Fentra's curse."

It wasn't fair of her to say that. And it couldn't be true.

I wouldn't let them be true.

~   ~   ~

The faint scent of smoke stirred my senses as I started south for the day, assuring me that I really was nearing the Iron Towers. The air had grown steadily warmer with each passing day and heavy rains had turned the ground into a soggy morass that squelched beneath my feet with every step and left my clothes in a permanent state of dampness. Green shoots of new grass sprang up from the spongy earth and the handful of shrubs and bushes and spindly trees that fought for their place among the windswept plains were showing green and pink buds.

My boots were nothing more than bits of leather held together by a few threads here and there. The lacings that were supposed to tie them up around my leg had broken off, leaving the shaft of the boots to flap loose around my leg. Holes had worn through the knees of my pants. A more ragged sight, I'm not sure I could have made. Mother would have been appalled.

The thought of my mother lent a little extra strength and speed to my steps as the sun rose higher and the smell of smoke grew stronger. It was still too early in the spring for most of the tribes to dare venturing out into the plains again. Late snowstorms were deadly and not to be risked when there was safety to be had.

I'd walked only about an hour before the smoke was no longer just a scent but a sight, a hazy smear against the blue sky. Then it was near enough that I could make out the fire and two or three figures sitting around it as well as a line of three horses picketed to the ground. I dropped to my knees and then to my stomach, watching the first people I'd seen in weeks. Watching, because I wasn't sure if I dared approach them.

Roving bands of outcasts usually braved the early spring in hopes of getting a head start on the best hunting but two or three people were hardly enough to make up a band of outcasts. Which meant that the small group in front of me then was most likely a scouting party for a tribe. Most tribes sent out their tracker and one or two others to watch the herds' movements. Most tribes would offer hospitality, at least initially, to anyone who wandered into their midst.

Most.

There were at least four tribes that I never wanted to have any dealings with again - the four that had thought to capture me and wring their futures out of me before Drakkus.

Lying there as mud seeped its way inside my very worn clothes, I watched, trying to search for some clue that would reveal their identity, but the distance was too far. I didn't relish the idea of crawling through the mud to get near enough, either. Nor, in the vast nothingness of the plains, was there a way around them unless I was willing to go several hours out of the way.

Torn between a sudden longing to see and speak to anyone but myself and a wariness that Drakkus and Brym had begun in me, I might have spent the entire morning trying to decide my next step if one of the distant figures hadn't stood and started in my direction.

It shouldn't have taken me by surprise. If there was a tracker among the party, they would have felt my approach even at that distance. But my heart began to thump hard against my chest, making it difficult to draw in a soft, steady breath.

There was nowhere to run.

Nowhere to hide.

No chance of being missed.

And all I could think of in that moment as the stranger approached was Drakkus' tether and Brym's chain. I never wanted to feel either ever again. Drakkus' words of warning when he said I would never be safe again flashed through my mind.

With only a few minutes to decide anything, I remembered what I'd told Rensi. I had no intention of being anyone else's prisoner. And I certainly didn't have any intention of lying still and waiting. I pulled myself up out of the mud that sucked me down, got to my feet and ran.

My feet sank several inches with each step, the soggy ground slowing me down. Weeks of living off of only what I could hunt with my knives didn't help me either. Nor did my tattered and quickly falling apart boots. I tripped and stumbled along, barely keeping my balance. It was a race I knew was lost long before the footsteps coming up behind caught up with me and an arm snaked around my chest, pulling me to an abrupt stop.

I squirmed, twisting around in my new captor's arm. A knife was already gripped firmly in my hand. A knife I'd only used against animals. I pulled my arm back to slash with it, but my captor's free hand clamped around my wrist, freezing it in place.

"Korris?"

The voice was familiar. The way it said my name told me I was familiar to them. I lifted my eyes and gasped. The knife slid free of my grip, dropping to the soggy ground with a soft splash. Relief flooded through me so hard and fast, I was left breathless.

"Jarris?"

My older brother's arm released me, and I stumbled away a little as he stepped back to look down at me. He stood head and shoulders above me, a trait he'd inherited from our father. His face, as thin and lean as the rest of him, broke into a grin that was equal parts troubled and happy. He shook his head, his eyes traveling over me, taking in my torn and tattered clothing. "You look terrible."

"Do you have any food?"

Jarris laughed, the sound of it deeper than I remembered it being. "I have food. But it's going to take more than food to make you look any better. Thank the

Fates you're alive, though. Mother's been worried out of her mind all winter. It was all we could do to keep her from setting off after you all by herself."

I fell in step beside him with his arm slung over my shoulder, as we made our way back to the fire, trying to calm the wild racing of my heart. I'd made it. Whether by the Fates' hands or by pure chance, I'd made it. Nothing else mattered in light of that thought.

"What's happened to you?" Jarris asked as we neared the small camp and its only other occupant.

A chunk of meat hung on a spit over the fire, roasting slowly and filling the air with a scent that made me greedy for a taste of it. There'd been no fire for me, no cooked meat, while I'd crossed the plains. Not only did I have nothing to start a fire with, but I had feared drawing unwanted attention to myself. I hadn't realized just how much I'd missed the welcoming blaze of one until I saw Jarris'. Slipping out from underneath his arm, I hurried ahead of him to its side.

"Eat first. Then I'll tell you."

Jarris laughed again and I found myself joining in. It had been so long since I'd had reason to laugh that it felt strange just then. It sounded strange, too. High against Jarris' deep one. Belonging to someone that wasn't me.

Jarris' companion rose to his feet at our approach and looked me up and down. I recognized him at once. He was a man by the name of Gorrin, one of our tribe's best hunters, which made him a frequent companion of

Jarris'. The man looked between Jarris and me, raising his eyebrows in an unspoken question before realization crossed his face.

Gorrin dipped his head slightly. "You've found your way back to us, have you? Your father will be pleased."

Gorrin might have said more but a sign from my brother silenced him. I sat down and set myself to the task of eating enough to settle the gnawing hunger that I'd almost grown used to. Roast venison burned my hands and my mouth but that was not enough to slow me. I hadn't eaten my fill in so long. Jarris and Gorrin partook of the same meal with less relish than I did, stealing amused glances in my direction as I devoured the largest portion.

As I wiped the last bits of grease from my mouth with the back of my hand, Jarris gave Gorrin a look that sent the man off to a safe distance, ostensibly to stand guard. With Jarris' gift of tracking, the task was completely unnecessary, but it gave us privacy and I was thankful for it.

I let out a contented sigh as Jarris leaned forward and jabbed at the fire, stirring it up into a comforting blaze.

"So, what happened?" he asked, his voice quiet, his dark eyes searching my face. "No one's ever dared to take you for so long."

I blew out a long breath and turned to gaze out at the empty plains around us. The sky above us had turned to a heavy gray, giving the entire scene a sort of bleak appearance but it was better than facing my brother. Jarris had a way of staring that made one feel as if he could look straight through them. That was another trait he'd inherited from our father. Lies never got past him, nor did half-truths. I didn't wish to lie to my brother but trying to put several months' worth of time into a single conversation was daunting.

"If it makes it easier, we already know who took you," Jarris said, a half-smile breaking up the intensity of his stare a little.

"Drakkus' man reached you?"

Jarris let out a derisive snort. "Of course he did. We weren't hard to find. Not that Father listened to a word he said about going south."

"Did Father..."

"Father got what he needed from the man. But that was months ago. What's happened since?"

It took more than a moment to collect my thoughts and force them into cooperation, but I began. I began with the night Drakkus' men slipped inside our elder's yurt. When I'd woken to being rolled over onto my stomach by strange hands, a gag forced between my teeth and my hands yanked behind me and bound tightly.

Bit by agonizing bit, I told Jarris all that had transpired since my capture. He listened well, not interrupting until I told him of the attack of Brym's men on Drakkus' camp and of how Drakkus died and of the tether that Rensi had transferred to herself instead of breaking.

"But Korris," he said, a confused frown on his face, "tethers don't work if the person dies."

"Maybe they don't most of the time."

"Never."

"But it did," I protested. "I felt it."

Jarris opened his mouth, and I was quite sure he meant to argue the point, but he shut it a moment later and waved a hand for me to go on. Reluctant to leave the matter, I continued relating my tale and he continued listening, silent once more.

Even though I had no wish to lie to my brother, there were parts of my story that wouldn't be told. Parts that I was too ashamed of. Parts that were too painful to remember, even weeks or months later.

I think Jarris knew that I'd left out bits and pieces but since it had taken me well over an hour to share what I had, he didn't ask me any questions when I'd fallen silent. Instead, he just told me to sleep and assured me that we would start for the Iron Towers the following morning.

CHAPTER 2

I'D TOLD MYSELF THAT I would never walk time again.

It was a promise I'd made when I first left Dragon's Nest and Brym behind me.

I broke that promise.

Curiosity drove me to it. Curiosity awakened by Jarris' claim. I'd promised myself I would never do it again but a promise to yourself is an easy thing to break.

I waited until Jarris and Gorrin thought me asleep and there was no risk of them trying to speak to me. Then I let my mind wander back to the day of the attack on Drakkus' camp. Pulling up the memory, I let it replay itself in my mind, sifting through the threads of all the people there until I found Drakkus'. I saw him go down, three arrows piercing him. I saw the pure white snow beneath him turn red and melt with the warmth of his blood as it flowed unabated. Rensi was at his side, her words muted, but her tears quite visible.

When Rensi was dragged away, fighting still, I forced my sight to remain with Drakkus. His body lay inert in the snow, no sign of life showing itself.

Many long hours he lay there, unmoving. I was tempted to withdraw from his thread and return to the present as I felt the pain building inside my head. I would have if it hadn't been for Rayka and Otho's appearance as the sun disappeared behind the western horizon. I watched as Rayka knelt beside her husband and...

"Korris, get up." Jarris' sharp voice and rough shaking pulled me out of my time walking and back into the present.

He didn't wait for any response from me before hauling me to my feet and shoving me in the direction of their horses. I stumbled, as unfocused as if he'd just awakened me from a deep sleep.

"What's going on?"

"Something's out there. Something I don't recognize. We need to go."

Gorrin was already mounted and holding the reins of the other two horses, only one of which was saddled. Jarris pushed me toward the saddled horse. I slipped my foot into the stirrup just as a howl shattered the night air around us.

A howl I'd heard before.

My blood ran ice cold in my veins, a shiver walking down my spine at the sound of it. I thought I'd left all that behind me in Dragon's Nest.

"That's an..."

"A what? What is it?" Jarris' voice was tight, an edge to each word he spoke. I'd never heard him sound like that before. He was on his own horse already, sitting its bare back with ease.

Another howl. Closer. Louder.

"An Outlander," I whispered.

The words were barely out of my mouth before all three of us were moving, the horses beneath us spurred into a gallop by their own terror rather than our command. I rode between Gorrin and Jarris, clinging to my reins and a handful of my mount's mane as its hooves pounded into the wet ground beneath me. The headache that my time walking had left with me made the world feel as if it were spinning around me and I gritted my teeth against the nausea it called up.

"There's only one," Jarris shouted to Gorrin over the thunder of the horses' hooves and the howling of the beast somewhere behind us. "If we separate, we might throw it off. Ride for the Iron Towers. If you get there first, tell my father that Korris is found, and the rumors are true."

Gorrin didn't answer. He just tugged his horse to one side and moments later, he was out of sight, lost in the darkness of night. My thought in that moment proved that I was as much a coward then as I had been in Dragon's Nest when faced with an impossible choice. I wanted the creature to hunt Gorrin and not us. I never wanted to be near another Outlander for as long as I lived.

"Faster," Jarris called out from beside me.

I leaned forward, digging my heels into my horse's sides but I didn't think I could make it run faster than it already was. Already, its sides were heaving, and flecks of white lather were visible on its neck.

The splash of feet hitting the saturated ground behind us told me that the monster still gave chase, that it had picked us as its targets and not Gorrin. My heart, already stuck in my throat, lurched at the sound of its nearness.

"*Time walker*," a hiss came through the dark. A voice that went straight to my ears and sent a quiver of terror through me such as I'd never had before. It was Brym's voice. And it was coming from behind us. "*Time walker.*"

I risked a glance in Jarris' direction, but he didn't seem to be aware of the voice. His gaze was straight ahead, focused on where we were running.

It was a voice meant only for me. And I had the sinking feeling that the beast was meant only for me, as well. It wouldn't hunt Gorrin down instead of us because Gorrin wasn't the one it had been sent for. And even as the realization sank into me, it didn't make sense.

Brym was dead.

I'd watched her die, and I'd watched her body dissolve into dust within minutes. Perhaps she'd already given her command for the Outlanders to hunt me down if I escaped.

However it came to be, it chased us, and we fled. Darkness concealed it from us. Aside from its occasional howl, our only clue that it still followed was the sound of its running feet. Whichever monster it was, it couldn't catch our horses, but it could keep up with them. We pressed our mounts harder and harder, driving them to the end of their strength as the hours of the night wore on, bringing us closer to dawn.

Dawn was our savior.

The sun came up and, in its light, the Outlander vanished. Where it went, I had no idea. There was no place to hide in the plains. But it was gone. And not a moment too soon. My horse tripped, stumbling over its own trembling legs. Jarris' horse was no better than mine. I don't think even terror could have coerced another sprint out of either of them.

Jarris dropped to the ground and knelt, placing his hand against the driest spot of soil he could reach.

"I don't feel it anymore," he said after a moment of concentration. "We'll walk for a bit."

I slid down and landed on nearly numb legs and feet. Beside me, my horse huffed and snorted, head hanging low. It took more than one tug of the reins to drag the beast into a walk beside me.

Every few minutes, Jarris would squint up at where the sun was still young in the sky.

"That thing chased us the wrong way," he said. "We've gone west when we should have gone south."

I was too tired to give it much thought, my own head drooping as much as my horse's. I should have slept when I had the chance rather than walk time. It hadn't even given me the answer I wanted because Jarris had pulled me back into the present too soon. When I thought about it, I wasn't even sure why I'd been so curious. It didn't matter to me whether Drakkus lived or died. Perhaps if I'd still been with Rensi, I could have given her an assurance one way or the other.

Jarris corrected our course, turning us south once more. It took more than an hour of walking before the horses' breath steadied and the sweat that caked their sides dried. It took almost as much time for my heart to slow down. Jarris stopped often, putting a hand to the ground and each time withdrawing it with a shake of his head. The trouble that haunted his eyes deepened each time.

"How does it just disappear?" I heard him mutter.

Even though I knew he hadn't meant for me to hear, I shrugged in response. Jarris missed the gesture and continued on, leaving me to my own thoughts.

I wondered which Outlander it was. If it was the monstrous beast that had killed Alkan or if it was the one that carried plague with it. Perhaps neither. There'd been hundreds trapped in cages beneath Dragon's Nest and I hadn't taken the time to get a good look at any of them. I'd been far too busy running for my life.

"I suppose we ought to stop and rest," Jarris said when the sun was high above our heads. "It hasn't been near us for hours now."

"I don't think they like light. Maybe it's just waiting until night to hunt again."

"All the more reason to rest now."

Since it had been more than a day since I'd slept, I wasn't about to argue with him.

~ ~ ~

For three days, we followed the same pattern. For three days, the Outlander disappeared at the coming of the sun only to close in on us again as soon as the darkness came. For three nights it whispered the same words, *Time walker.*

I kept that voice and its whispered words to myself, half believing that it was only my imagination by the time the sun rose each day. Jarris said little to me, but his face was drawn a little more each morning when the creature abandoned its chase and he realized it had driven us west again.

"If we just had firedust, we could kill it," I said to him on that third morning, when he rose from his tracking and shook his, his troubled frown the deepest I'd seen it yet. Exhaustion colored the skin under his eyes the shade

S. T. Hobbs

of a darkening bruise. I wasn't sure if he slept while I did or not.

"Firedust," Jarris repeated the word quietly. "What is it? And you're sure that's what it takes?"

"I don't know if it's the only thing that kills them, but it does kill them. They had it in Dragon's Nest." And we'd used it to burn half of Dragon's Nest to the ground.

Jarris fell silent for some time after that brief exchange and I knew my brother well enough to not try to speak again. He preferred silence when he was trying to think. He did not speak again until we stopped to rest in the afternoon.

"We're closer to Abirell than we are to the Iron Towers by now," he said. His words took me so completely by surprise that I choked on the water I was drinking, going into a fit of coughing that lasted several minutes. He watched me curiously. "They would have this firedust, I think, since they are a gateway."

"No," I said flatly when I'd recovered enough to speak.

"Korris, whatever this thing is, we can't outrun it and we can't seem to find a way to mislead it. If anything, it is misleading us. Our best chance is to kill it and you're the one who said firedust is the way to do that."

"We can't go to Abirell."

"Korris..."

"I can't." I was beginning to regret not telling him about the part I'd played in Abirell's coming demise, but I was still too ashamed to say the words. What would

Jarris think of me if he knew how weak I'd been? If he knew that I'd sacrificed thousands of people just to spare myself and a handful of others? "I just... Why can't we just keep trying to reach the Iron Towers?"

Jarris rubbed a weary hand over his face, and I knew from the sigh that slipped out of him that his temper, usually so well controlled, was fraying. He was exhausted. Waving a dismissive hand in my direction, he said, "Just rest. We'll talk about it later."

I made no move to lay down although my body longed for the opportunity to relax. "Have you slept at all since that thing started hunting us?"

"It's fine, Korris. Just..."

"Let me stay up and watch." He shook his head, but I went on, "Jarris, I can do it. I've been fending for myself for months now. I've crossed the plains by myself, and I haven't gotten eaten alive yet. Staying up and keeping watch is nothing compared to that. I can do it."

He wavered at my argument, doubt creeping into his eyes. Doubt, and an undeniable need for sleep. "I suppose you did. What about if you have a vision?"

"I can feel them coming before I actually have one. If I start to feel one coming, I'll wake you. I promise. But you can't just not sleep for days and days at a time."

It was his own desperate need for sleep that persuaded him more than any argument I made. Under any other circumstances, I was quite sure my older brother would never have agreed to allow me to shoulder the responsibility of keeping watch. I was almost glad that necessity had forced him to do so now. I was almost glad of the chance to prove to him that I was as capable as he always had been.

He was asleep within moments, though, revealing just how great his need was.

In the stillness that surrounded me, Rensi's words came back. Her voice in my head haunting me with an accusation I could neither accept nor fully deny - *You are Fentra's curse.*

I didn't want to be.

Chapter 3

~**Rensi's Writings**~

I'VE REACHED HOME AT LAST *and I never thought I'd be so happy to see a place in all my life. Not a single person recognized me when I first managed to drag myself through the gates and up to the palace. I suppose I shouldn't have expected them to.*

It has been three years since Father took us with him to the plains. Three years and what do I have to show for it?

Dirt. A lot of dirt.

I feel as if I've carried half the plains into Ludys with me. So it's really no wonder that the gallants at the front gate of the palace tried to turn me away. Thank the Fates old Horquim had more sense than the gallants at the gate and managed to see past my filth and rags, even if it did take him several minutes.

Now that I've had a nice, long, hot bath and Naloni has burned my old rags, I'm beginning to feel more like a human and less like one of those plains' savages we've lived amongst for the last three years. My cousin, Jahniss, has even lent me some of her own clothes until I can have new ones made. Real smooth, soft fabric and not rough leather! I almost cried, I was so happy just at the feel of them.

All those weeks trying to get here, I did nothing but worry about what Uncle Mitkas would say when I arrived. After the way things happened between him and Father, I half expected him to turn me away at the gates and banish me from Ludys. I'm not sure what I would have done then.

Mother always said that Ludys was where we would meet again if ever we were separated. She and Otho haven't made it yet, and I'm trying hard not to worry over that. Uncle Mitkas allayed all my worries about his reception at once. He sent word just as soon as I'd been brought to my old room saying that he bore none of us any ill will and wished things had happened differently and was sorry that I'd been forced to return in such a manner.

I saw Uncle Mitkas just as soon as I was clean enough to brave leaving the privacy of my room (which he has generously allowed me to return to) and I have to admit I wasn't ready for having to tell of Father's death. I've tried my best not to think of that day.

And I've tried my best not to think about how Kor could have warned us but didn't. I tell myself he was right. I try to make myself believe that. But I just can't. Not when it cost Father his life. Not after everything that happened to us in Dragon's Nest.

I hate him when I think of those things and I know it's not fair because we were the ones to take him from his family and his home. I hate him for leaving me, too. That's not fair, either, I suppose.

And I'm sure he hates me just as much, especially after what I said to him last. Perhaps I shouldn't have said it. The look he gave me was so awful when I said it, his face almost as white as the ash still stuck in his black hair. I suppose I would have looked at someone the same if they'd said something like that to me.

Uncle Mitkas asked me all about Kor, too, of course. Perhaps I ought to be a little ashamed - after how kind and generous he's been - for leaving out a few details. It just didn't seem like a good idea to go spilling my ideas about Fentra and her curse and Kor's part in it all. I hope I'm wrong about it, anyway. I don't think he wishes to be her curse but I'm not sure he actually has any choice in the matter.

I did tell Uncle Mitkas all about what happened to Dragon's Nest and he's promised to send some of our soldiers to ensure there is no breach made by the Outlanders. It was such a relief for him to decide that.

Ever since I saw Dragon's Nest go up in flames, all I could think about was how the Outlanders could get inside now. Hopefully, Uncle Mitkas' men will reach Dragon's Nest before the Outlanders have gained too much of a foothold. We've never had to fight them on this side of the mountains and I'm not sure we have much chance of winning if we must.

Chapter 4

WE SHOULDN'T GO TO ABIRELL," I said once again as Jarris kept us moving in a steady westward direction. "The Iron Towers would be better."

Jarris stopped walking, his shoulders rising and then falling as he took a sharp breath. "Why? Why, Korris? You keep saying we shouldn't go to Abirell, but you won't say why. Have you foreseen something?"

He wasn't facing me, so he missed the small nod I gave in answer to his question. It wasn't often Jarris lost control of his temper. It was even less often that he lost control of his temper with me. The last time that had happened was more than a year before, on one of the rare occasions my father allowed me to go hunting. Jarris had taken me, and I had ruined his hunt by tripping over some vermin's hole in the ground and frightening our prey away.

But, from the rigid line of his back now and the way he wouldn't turn to look at me and the tight edge to his voice, I knew he was at least frustrated.

"Well?" he asked, when I didn't answer right away.

"We just shouldn't. I did see something and I don't know when it will happen but I know it will be soon and we shouldn't be there. I don't want to be there when it happens." I didn't want to be there to see when the information I'd given Brym turned into reality.

His shoulders slumped forward a bit and he ran his hand over his face and up into his hair. He'd done the same thing at least five times in the same number of minutes.

Six days of trying to stay ahead of the Outlander was wearing on all of us - even the horses. Their heads were always drooping, their footsteps plodding. Terror made them run at night but in the day we had to resort to all sorts of tricks to keep them walking until their breathing at least evened out a bit. The food and water Jarris and Gorrin had packed was running low and we had no opportunity to replace it.

"What did you see?"

I'd kept the list of people I told my visions to very short in the years that I'd had them. Father, Mother, our tribe's elder, and then Drakkus and Brym. I'd never confided one in Jarris. He'd never asked.

"There's going to be plague there."

"Plague? We haven't had that in... well, we haven't had it in three hundred years at least. Are you sure that's what you saw?"

"I'm sure," I said softly.

Jarris continued on in the same direction as if I hadn't just warned him of the imminent death that awaited Abirell. Arguing further would only have provoked his anger. I tugged on my horse's reins and followed, trying to ignore the sick feeling in the pit of my stomach and wondering what other words I could speak that would convince my brother to turn south once more.

~   ~   ~

My eyelids refused to obey me and slid shut over and over with stubborn defiance. I pinched the skin on my arm and twisted it hard, hoping the pain would jolt me awake enough to take control of myself. A few feet away from me, Jarris lay asleep. He kept watch two days to my one, insisting that he needed less sleep than I and that we'd reach Abirell, and safety, soon.

The pain my own fingers had caused on my arm was little more than a niggling sensation of discomfort, not enough to break the hold of exhaustion on me. I felt myself giving in to sleep even as I fought it, the daylight fading from my eyes as they shut without permission once more.

The cold kiss of sharp iron against my throat did what pain could not. I snapped my head up only to have a hand clamped over my mouth and my body hauled up from the ground.

Perhaps it ought to have bothered me that my first thought in that moment was not fear for my life, but rather fear that Jarris would never trust me to keep watch again. I'd failed his trust in me. I didn't even struggle against the imprisoning hands, although I did still try to call out a muffled warning to Jarris. The sour taste of sweaty skin filled my mouth as my tongue brushed against the man's hand, but I'd made enough noise to wake Jarris.

My brother was on his feet faster than the three men who circled around from behind me could get hold of him, a long, vicious looking blade in his hand. The three men approaching him froze, none of them wishing to be the first to feel the edge of that blade.

If they'd known my brother at all, they would have known that all three of them would be dead within moments if they took another step toward him. Jarris had made hunting his life from the first time he'd learned he was a tracking. Where others did it as a means to survive, he had honed it into a skill that was unrivaled by anyone I'd ever met. I'd never seen anyone else kill with as much speed or efficiency.

He stood there, a casualness in his posture that belied the same kind of coiled anticipation a viper might have before striking out at its victim.

The knife pressed deeper into the soft skin of my throat, stinging a little as I felt a warm trickle of blood escape a vein. I swallowed hard against its pressure.

"You don't want to kill him," Jarris said, an edge to his voice that the others seemed to miss. I pitied the men if they did kill me. Jarris' efficiency could be cruel when he wanted it to be. "He's the oracle and if you kill him this all starts all over again."

For a long, stretched out moment, there was no response. Then the knife lifted a little and the deep voice of the man holding me filled my ears. "Peace, stranger. We've no wish to kill either of you."

"Yes, the knife at his throat makes your words very convincing," Jarris said.

The knife fell away completely, and I drew in a breath, reaching up with one hand to feel the nick it had left behind. The man holding me made no effort to stop my movement.

"Just a bit of caution. You are strangers to Abirell, and these are not the sort of days that we can allow strangers to wander unchecked into our lands. What's your purpose here?"

"We came to seek the protection of Abirell, not its hurt."

"Protection from what?" The man released his hold on me entirely and I stepped quickly forward and to the side, out of his reach should he change his mind. If Jarris still planned on killing him, he had his chance then.

Jarris, however, sheathed his own knife, and said, "We've been hunted by an Outlander for more than a week now. It's driven us this way every night. Korris," he gestured toward me, "said firedust can kill it and so we've come here in hopes that Abirell has firedust."

I glanced around at the men, trying to read their intentions from their faces. Not one of the four was clothed above the waist, their skin tanned deep enough that I assumed what little they wore was their usual attire. And although all of them carried long knives, none were drawn from the sheaths that hung from their belts. The three who'd moved toward Jarris had turned to watch the man beside me. That, and the fact that he was the only one who spoke, marked him as their leader. Nothing else about his appearance did.

"So, the rumors are true? The Outlanders have breached the barrier?"

"At least one has."

More silence, more potent than it had been before. The leader turned to me and studied me with a curiosity that lacked any greed or malice. I wasn't used to that from people who had newly discovered my gift, but I tensed anyway, wishing Jarris had said nothing of my gift to those men.

"And he is really the oracle?" he asked Jarris, still studying me with something akin to awe on his face.

"Yes." Oracle, time walker. Never just Korris. Always my gift.

"Come. If we move quickly, we can be within Abirell before nightfall. We shall see if this Outlander will follow you there. And if it does, we have more than enough firedust to deal with it." He held out his arm and Jarris clasped it in brief greeting. "Name's Orle."

One of the men reached for our horses' reins and the other two started off in the lead as Jarris introduced both himself and me. Orle looked me over once more and nodded. "Semptius will want to see him."

"Who's that?" I asked, tired of being spoken about as if I wasn't standing right there. My heart had a wild flutter in its beating and a familiar band of tightness settled over my chest.

"The governor of Abirell," Orle answered, giving me an almost stunned expression that made me wonder what it was about my question that had been so shocking.

The tightness in my chest grew stronger, making my breath rapid and shallow. I swallowed hard and tried to catch Jarris' eyes as much to convey my deep distrust of the situation as to avoid Orle's intense gaze.

"We can find our own way there. Can't we, Jarris?" My voice was higher than usual, and I'd taken a step back, away from the entire group.

Jarris raised a bewildered eyebrow at my question and shrugged one shoulder. "Why would we?"

Because I knew where this would end. Because I didn't want any more tethers or chains. Because I didn't want to become anyone else's game piece. Because I didn't want to be picked apart and used anymore. And surely the governor of Abirell would do all those things.

Why had Jarris even told them what I was? I fought my rapid breathing, trying to calm it. All that my effort accomplished was making me lightheaded and queasy. With a start, I realized that my hands were balled into tight fists at my sides, clenched so hard that no blood could flow to my fingertips.

"Come on, Korris. We want to get there before dark," Jarris said.

Jarris didn't know. He couldn't have known. His own gift made him valuable to our tribe but not beyond it. There were other trackers, enough that one was not special. And if he sided with the men of Abirell, there really wasn't anything I could do to prevent the inevitable.

Lowering my head to hide the paleness of my face, I started after the others, acutely conscious of the way Orle continued to watch me. I wasn't sure what he expected to see. Every time I'd opened my mouth he stared as if it were the most remarkable thing in the world. Perhaps he'd thought oracles didn't speak unless prophecy of the future.

"We'll be safe, Korris," Jarris said quietly as he walked beside me. He gave me a smile that I'm sure was meant to be reassuring but he didn't understand. "You'll see. Abirell's known for being a courteous and welcoming city."

I looked over my shoulder and found Orle watching me as carefully as ever and I said nothing to my brother.

"You are no longer safe," Drakkus had said to me all those long months before. As I walked toward Abirell, toward another leader who would likely wish to have his piece of me, I wondered how many times I would have to prove his words true.

Chapter 5

ABIRELL WAS A CITY OF WOOD.

Wooden houses. Wooden palisade. Wooden watchtowers.

Abirell was a city of many smells. Sea salt and water. Fish. Seaweed. Wood. A strange mingling of both pleasant and noxious odors that was distinct to Abirell.

The sun had sunk low in the sky, slipping behind the wooden outline of the city, turning the silhouette of the city black and coloring the silver sea beyond it bright shades of orange and yellow. We were within reach of the city gates. Full darkness, and with it the Outlander's return, was still at least an hour off. Wooden watchtowers stood at intervals along the plains' side of the city, and I could see the helmeted heads of the watchmen peering over their protective walls. Two of those watchtowers flanked a gate made of thick wooden beams and bound in heavy strips of iron.

"You've a great many men on duty," Jarris commented as we got near enough to see the many bobbing heads that moved behind the palisade and inside the watch towers.

"Semptius ordered it so when we first heard rumors of a breach in the barrier. It is for our safety, nothing more."

A tingling in my right hand distracted me from following any more of their conversation. I uncurled my clenched fingers slowly, feeling the blood rush into them after being restricted for so long. With that rush of blood, warm sticky moisture filled my palm, and I brought my hand up to look at it.

I stared for a long moment before realizing what was happening. The scar Borssa's knife had left in my hand wept blood. Not much, but it shouldn't have bled at all. I frowned and stopped walking without realizing it as I stared down at it, trying to make sense of what my eyes saw.

It had been healed.

Fully sealed and nothing more than a pale, slightly raised scar. It had not bled since that first week in Dragon's Nest when Brym had picked, fascinated, at it. Perhaps I had dug my own fingernails into my own palm harder than I thought. The tingling inside the old wound turned warm and pulsing.

"Come on, Korris. We're almost there," Jarris said, giving me a light shove on the shoulder to get me moving again. He'd misread the cause of my stop and I shut my hand into a fist again so that he wouldn't see the real reason.

We paused outside the shut gates while Orle went ahead of us and spoke to the gatekeepers. Whatever he said to them made them all turn and look in our direction.

At me.

He had told them about me, about what I was. I lowered my head and took a small step back to stand partially shielded behind my brother.

"Welcome to Abirell," Orle said as he guided us through the gates that shut as soon as we were through.

The words rang through me, setting off a memory of Rensi and I's arrival at Dragon's Nest. Harysh had said the same words to us then and they had heralded the beginning of the worst few months I'd ever lived through. I drug my feet through the dirt of the street as Jarris' presence behind me kept me moving forward.

"Whatever Outlander hunted you here cannot breach our defenses. You'll be safe so long as you choose to stay," Orle continued, leading the way down the wide street that the gate had dumped us onto.

There was an unnatural hush hanging over the city. Faces peered out at us from behind curtained windows but almost no one was out in the streets. It seemed odd that everyone had taken to their houses before the sun was fully down but since I'd never been inside a city like Abirell before, I wasn't sure. On the plains, we generally stayed up well after the setting sun, gathered around our fires, either listening to our elder tell stories of days gone by or exchanging our own stories.

For the first time since he'd agreed to come, Jarris seemed to acquire some of my apprehension. He put a hand on my shoulder and stopped me. "Thank you for your kindness in bringing us safely into the city, but I think we can make our own way from here."

Orle stopped and turned, confusion wrinkling the weathered skin of his face. "Semptius will want to speak to him," he gestured toward me, "as soon as possible. And I have no doubt he'll offer you both lodging for however long you need it. The great house has more than enough room for you."

"We can find our own lodging."

I wasn't sure how Jarris would do that or how he knew how to do that. I certainly didn't. We did everything so differently in the plains.

The confused wrinkles on Orle's face deepened for a moment before smoothing out with the light of understanding. "You have nothing to fear from Semptius. He will merely wish to ask for the particulars regarding your chase by the Outlander. And, of course, he will find great interest in meeting the oracle. Anyone would."

We couldn't have truly resisted if we wanted to. Jarris' ferocity in a fight was no match for the number of armed men within easy reach. The sick feeling in my gut grew stronger and cold sweat mingled with the warm blood on the palm of my hand. In the silence that hung over the streets of Abirell, I was quite sure the rapid pounding of my heart was audible to the others.

"Very well. Lead on," Jarris said after a moment.

I glanced at him as he walked beside me. His face had returned to its careful mask of indifference, but his eyes didn't stop moving, taking in everything as we passed, searching for threats in the shadows.

The wide road we followed from the gate led straight through the city. In the lengthening shadows of the evening, I peered down the much narrower streets that stemmed from it. Thanks to the dusk, not much was visible, but I did wonder how the people of Abirell could abide being so crowded together. Some of the houses stood so close to each other that their residents could likely reach out of their windows or front doors and hold hands if they wanted to.

Along the road we followed, the fronts of the buildings rose up high on either side of us, blocking out much of the sky except what was directly overhead. From many of those tall buildings, wooden signs with colored markings on them swung, creaking in the gentle breeze that blew in from the sea.

My curiosity as Orle led us through the city was enough to almost make me forget my dread.

When the road came to an abrupt end in front of a massive, sprawling building, that dread came rushing back. My gaze traveled up the front of the building. It wasn't as tall as some of the others we'd passed but the length of it made up for it, turning it into an imposing sight.

It had many windows, most of which were spilling light outside. There was no wall around it, no gate to pass through. Orle led us straight up to the front doors and knocked. The doors were made from a solid piece of wood each, with iron work designs overlaid.

From inside, a latch lifted, and the doors were opened, creaking softly on their hinges. The golden glow of many candles poured out of the opening and into the growing darkness, silhouetting the one who'd opened the door and making it impossible to see their face.

Orle stepped inside and we, not having much choice left in the matter, followed. The three men who'd accompanied Orle remained outside.

"Please inform Governor Semptius that I've brought visitors to see him and that we'll be awaiting his presence in the great hall," Orle said to the woman who'd allowed us in. She bowed her head slightly and left to convey that message.

Orle led us in the opposite direction, taking us to a room I could only assume was the great hall. Not a word passed between the three of us as we stopped inside it and waited.

I stood there, shifted from one foot to the other, trying to convince myself that Abirell would end differently than Dragon's Nest. Trying to convince myself that not everyone would do what Brym had done to me.

~   ~   ~

The man who entered the great hall nearly an hour after Orle had led us into it was younger than I'd imagined a governor being. He could not have lived more than thirty winters. The only difference in dress between him and Orle was a loose, open shirt that left his chest and stomach exposed and instead of boots on his feet, he wore thin cloth slippers. His face was clean shaven with freckles all over. An unruly mop of brown hair bounced a little on top of his head with each step he took.

He hurried across the great length of the room, passing its three enormous fireplaces and motioning us to a long narrow table that took up the center of the room. High, straight backed wooden chairs lined both sides of the table, with a particularly large one sitting at the head.

"Captain Orle, I do hope you've a most pressing reason to intrude upon my solitude this evening," Semptius said, speaking quickly and clipping off each word as if it tasted sour in his mouth. He moved to the large chair at the head of the table and dropped into the seat with equal haste and complete disregard for his own person, drumming his fingers on the tabletop. His gaze darted from Orle to Jarris and I and he squinted as he looked us over. "What is this?"

"With all due respect, governor, I did not think you would wish to wait for morning before discovering the oracle's presence in our city nor did I think you wanted me to withhold the news that these two brought with them regarding an Outlander."

"Oracle? Outlander?" Semptius' fingers drilled the table in a rapid staccato that almost matched the rhythm of my heart. His face fell into a quick frown. Thin lips became thinner as he pressed them tightly together. One corner of his mouth twitched upward in a nervous spasm. "Where is this oracle?"

Orle gestured to me with a slight inclination of his head.

Semptius turned his entire chair so that the side of it was up against the table and stared at me hard, his eyebrows knitting together as he squinted across the distance. His fingers left off their tapping long enough for him to wave his hand, motioning me to come closer.

After hesitating a moment, I shuffled forward a few steps. In my mind, I already guessed what would eventually happen. Semptius wouldn't willingly allow me to leave Abirell. The next moment Jarris and I were left alone, I'd have to convince my brother to run with me - if we still could. For all I knew, Semptius was summoning me closer just so he could slip his tether on me.

"Come closer," Semptius said with another, less patient wave of his hand. "All the way over here if you please. My eyes are quite terrible at a distance."

I glanced over my shoulder at Jarris, hoping for some intervention or protest from him. He merely nodded. I crossed the open floor until I was standing in front of Semptius. His nose wrinkled up with disgust as he looked me up and down.

"Where was he found?"

"In the plains, just inside our border."

"Does he have a name? Something he goes by? Does he understand us?"

I swallowed down the growing edge of annoyance inside me, but the words still came out. "My name's Korris and I am capable of both understanding you and speaking for myself."

Semptius started, jerking back against his chair as if I'd just burned him. He took another fleeting moment to stare up at me before recovering himself and sitting up, adjusting the open shirt that hung from his shoulders. Behind the surprise in his light brown eyes, there was a hint of amusement.

"Yes, well, it has been a long time since we've had an oracle. A very long time. And there's been much speculation as to whether they were fully human or not."

"I'm human."

44

"Well, then," he gave me a crooked smile that was warm despite my misgivings, "the question is whether you're really the oracle, isn't it? But at this moment, I'm afraid a much more urgent and pressing question concerns the time of your last bath."

My face flushed hot, and I said nothing. He probably wouldn't have liked the answer to that question, anyway, since it had been months.

Semptius wasn't paying any more attention to me. He'd already jumped back into his conversation with Orle, asking him about the rumored Outlander. Orle explained what Jarris had said before. The news of an Outlander was apparently less shocking than news of an oracle. Semptius merely nodded his head along with each word that Orle spoke.

"Escort these two to their quarters. Then inform the men on watch tonight. If it's only one, it will be easily dealt with," Semptius said. He picked up a small bell that sat on the table and gave it a quick shake. A moment later the same woman who'd opened the front door for us appeared. "Balia, these two will be our guests for tonight. See to it that they are provided with rooms, whatever food they desire, and," he gave a pointed look in my direction, "a bath. Perhaps a change of clothes for this one if it can be managed."

Chapter 6

HOT WATER CLOSED IN AROUND me and I shut my eyes, laying the back of my head against the hard rim of the tub.

Jarris shouldn't have brought us to Abirell. But, surrounded by hot water, I couldn't work up any real annoyance at him for doing so. As the heat burrowed into me, stripping away the months of cold I'd endured, I could forget all about why I hadn't wanted him to bring us here.

For just that moment, I could forget the Outlander and the plague that was coming to Abirell. I could forget that I was the reason that plague was coming. I could forget the harrowing race Jarris and I had to run to reach the safety of Abirell and I could forget how much I wanted to get home to the rest of my family. I could forget what Semptius would demand from me to prove that I was truly the oracle or what he would do with me once he was sure that I was. I could forget about the blood still oozing out of the scar on my hand.

There was so much in my life that I wanted to forget.

For just that one moment, though, I savored the warmth and luxury of a hot bath - a luxury I'd never experienced before. In the plains, we bathed in whatever rivers or creeks were nearby, never in great tubs of heated water inside warm rooms. If Semptius was to be my new master, he at least offered me a comfort that neither Drakkus nor Brym ever gave me.

In the hallway outside my shut door, Jarris was deep in argument with Captain Orle. I wasn't sure what he was arguing about, but I'd known from the look on his face when Captain Orle escorted us to our room that he was upset. Perhaps because he'd been given no chance to partake in the conversation with Semptius or perhaps because he disliked the number of choices we were being given or rather, not being given.

The door opened and Jarris entered the room, shutting the door behind him and leaning back against it, preventing anyone from coming in behind him. He crossed his arms over his chest and stared past me, lost in thought.

"We should leave," I said, making a halfhearted effort to scrub my dirt encrusted skin with the brush I'd been given for the task. Balia had added flakes of dry, scented soap to the water that turned into a brown lather within moments. "We should slip out tonight before it's too late and get outside the walls, make our way to the Iron Towers."

My words pulled Jarris out of whatever reverie he was lost in, and he frowned. "Will you be alright in here by yourself tonight?"

"What?"

"If I leave you alone here tonight, will you be alright?"

I let the brush drop from my hand and it fell with a splash into the now murky water. "Didn't you hear what I just said? Did you listen to me at all?"

"Why are you so desperate to leave, Korris? You've been on the run for weeks. You haven't had proper food or rest or anything else for months. Don't you want to rest for a few days?"

Rather than answer him, I slunk further down into the water until it came up and touched my chin. I lifted my right hand enough to see that blood was still trickling from the cut and then I plunged it beneath the surface of the water, not wanting to think about why it was behaving like it was. The pulsing inside the cut had only grown stronger since our arrival at the governor's house, turning almost painful.

"Look, I know you're afraid of being here when the plague comes here, but it's not here yet and a day or two isn't going to hurt us. If anything, it'll be good for you," Jarris said, leaving his spot against the door and walking to the window instead. It was fully dark out by then and

I wasn't sure what Jarris was staring at so intently. "I want to join Captain Orle's men on the wall tonight. I'd like the chance to see this Outlander if I can. And I'd like to see how it's killed."

Of course, he did. Jarris had hunted every kind of prey that lived in the plains. Of course, he wanted the chance to hunt something different, something more formidable. It was who Jarris was. I could see the light of excitement in his eyes even if he tried to hide it for my sake.

Jarris wasn't used to being the one hunted. It had grated against him every night when we ran. In fact, if he hadn't felt responsible for taking care of me, I was quite sure he wouldn't have run at all. He would have tried to stand his ground and fight it. My presence had robbed him of that chance. Now he needed to be there when the roles shifted.

"If you'd rather..."

"Just go. We shouldn't leave until it's dead, anyway," I said glumly. It was true, too. I was desperate to get out of Abirell, but I wasn't in a hurry to put myself in the path of whatever creature had hunted us - hunted me. "I'll be fine for tonight."

Leaving the window, Jarris sat on the edge of the bed facing me. He pulled out one of his long, curved knives and ran his finger across its sharp edge, testing it.

"We'll leave in the morning if I know that thing is dead. How's that?"

"If they let me go."

"Of course, they'll let you go. Why wouldn't they? We're not their prisoners here."

"I'm the oracle, Jarris." I tipped my head back and shut my eyes. "Semptius won't let me go any more than Brym would. He's probably trying to think of how he can get a tether on me just as soon as possible so that I can't run even when I want to, just like Drakkus did. Or maybe he has a chain laying around that he'd prefer to use, like Brym did. Or some room he can keep me locked away in and only bring me out when he wants to know the future."

My brother looked truly mortified as the words spilled out of me, each so full of frustration and the constant undercurrent of fear that I'd stopped noticing but never stopped living with. Drakkus was right. I wasn't safe. I wasn't ever safe. And Jarris was only just realizing that. I wanted to say more, to make him realize more.

"I won't let him do that to you."

I blew out a breath that was almost a huff of laughter. "I doubt even you could stop him if that's what he wants."

Jarris stared down at the knife in his hands, his finger still running up and down the blade in a mindless motion. Several times he opened his mouth and then shut it again. Finally, he put the knife back into its sheath and pushed himself up to his feet.

"It's not safe for us to leave Abirell as long as that Outlander is out there. But as soon as it's dead, I'll come back here, and we'll leave. We'll sneak out if we have to."

He didn't wait for me to answer and all I could do anyway was nod. I heard the door shut softly behind him as he went to do the one thing he knew he was good at, the one thing he understood.

~   ~   ~

I was only halfway through the food Balia had kindly and silently left on a small trestle table in our room when I heard the quick, light footsteps coming down the hallway. They stopped in front of my door and a moment later, a series of rapid, staccato knocks rattled the door.

My mouth was too full of food to give an answer and I wasn't given time to anyway. The door swung open as if someone had kicked it and the first thing I saw as I tried to swallow down my entire mouthful of food in a single gulp was an armful of tomes and loose papers and scrolls all crammed together in a precarious stack that threatened to spill all over the threshold of my room. Behind that, Semptius' face peeked out at me.

"Good, you've bathed. And I see Balia found something clean for you to wear," he said as he came into the room and deposited his load on the large bed that I was looking forward to falling into just as soon as I'd eaten my fill. His intrusion quickly rearranged those plans.

I stared at the pile of books and writings and then up at him. My eyes followed his every move as he crossed to the trestle table, lifted the candle from it and used that flame to light every other candle in the room. The wax of the candles had a strange odor to it, almost as if it had spent so much time around fish that it had picked up the smell of them.

He had me alone. Jarris was gone to the palisade to watch for the Outlander. If Semptius was going to tether me, he had his chance. My chest contracted and my body tensed as I recalled that night when Drakkus had put his tether on me and the way it had felt, its presence seeping into my body, robbing me of my independence.

When the last candle was lit, Semptius turned to face me, a quizzical, crooked grin on his face. My apprehension must have been visible. His smile faltered a bit, and he held his hands, palms out, in front of him in a gesture of peace and harmlessness.

"No tether, Korris. No chains."

Heat flushed my face for a second time in front of the man.

"You will pardon us for being rather inquisitive hosts, but we do have terribly thin walls here and Captain Orle could not help but overhear your conversation with your brother."

"What do you want with me?" My appetite lost, I moved to sit on the edge of the bed, opposite all the books he'd dropped there and as far from him as I could comfortably get. The mattress sank and shifted beneath my weight, upsetting a stack of the books, and making them all slide down. The woolen blanket, thick and scratchy, bunched up in my fisted hands.

He blinked and frowned. "What do I want? Well, simply put, I would like to determine whether you are truly the oracle as you and your brother claim. You wouldn't believe the number of people who've claimed the same. Not one of them could see farther into the future than a fish could. And most wished to be compensated quite generously for their rather dubious services."

I wasn't sure what a fish had to do with seeing into the future. And I wasn't sure what he expected me to do to prove my gift. So, I said nothing and just continued to watch him.

Semptius paced the floor, his steps quick as he rubbed his hands together.

"I have to admit, you're the youngest that I've seen make that claim. There have been others as young as you but, of course, they all lived more than three hundred years ago. That," he gestured toward the pile on the bed, "is every written piece of knowledge we have of oracles here in Abirell. It's not much. The Iron Towers has a far greater collection of writings in their library, but they've rejected every offer I've made to get my hands on them. Queen Cholla is not an easy person to negotiate with and she does rather love her prized collection. They are rumored to have the only copy of the *Chronicles of Fentra*. Imagine what a tale that would be to read! A great deal of what we have here is nothing more than hearsay and speculation but from everything I have read you should be capable of seeing into the future at will. Is that true?"

It was the sort of question I did not wish to answer because I knew where it would inevitably lead and so I said nothing once more. If my silence irritated Semptius, he did not show it.

My eyes drifted to the pile, drawn by a helpless curiosity. I wondered what more Semptius could want when he had so much already. My fingers reached out and brushed against the soft, supple leather that bound one of the tomes. Golden marks were engraved on its cover, dulled by age and time. Certainly, it was more knowledge than I had known existed about oracles.

I wondered what secrets they contained, what truths they revealed. I wondered if any were written by oracles themselves, or if any of the past oracles had ever found themselves pulled from one captor to another. I wondered about the *Chronicles of Fentra* that he'd spoken of. My closest predecessor had been murdered, Drakkus had told me, and everyone had agreed that her death was for the best.

Semptius paused in his pacing and watched me curiously, apparently unoffended by my refusal to answer him. "You can read them if you like. I find the stories quite fascinating, myself, even if most of it is made up."

"No. I can't. I can't read."

"Ah, yes. I do forget how delinquent the plains' folk are in such matters," he said, thoughtless of how his words sounded to one of those "plains' folk". "Never mind, though. My purpose in bringing them was merely to compare your capabilities to those of oracles in the past. Although... Bless the Fates, you're bleeding everywhere!"

His exclamation startled me, and I withdrew my hand from the book. At first, I wasn't sure what he was talking about and then I remembered the cut on my hand. It was hardly bleeding everywhere but there was fresh blood smeared across both the palm and the back of my hand. Its persistence in bleeding for no reason was beginning to annoy me.

"Balia," he called out while I refrained from wiping the blood on my new, clean clothes. Turning back to me, he said, "You should have told me you were injured. I would have had it seen to immediately. I'm a terrible host leaving you untreated like this."

"It's nothing. I got the cut months ago. I'm not even sure what made it start bleeding now."

It was too late.

Balia was already in the room and Semptius was too busy telling her to find medicine and a bandage for my hand to listen to my protest. Balia said nothing, just ducking her head in a quick compliant nod. She returned within moments, sat beside me on the bed, and held out her hand expectantly. With a sigh, I laid my hand in hers and resigned myself to her care. It was hardly the most difficult thing I'd had to do.

Semptius stood over me, watching.

"Peculiar," he said, leaning close to get a good view of the old wound after Balia had wiped away the fresh blood. "Most peculiar."

Semptius stepped away then, one hand stroking his chin as he resumed his restless pacing. Before he could continue any conversation, the deep resonating clap of a large bell filled the night air.

Turning to me, Semptius gave me the same quizzical, lopsided smile I'd seen before.

"It seems your Outlander has arrived."

CHAPTER 7

~Rensi's Writings~

*E*VERY DAY THAT PASSES WITH *no sign or word of Mother and Otho leaves me closer and closer to despair. It makes me question whether Mother really told us to return to Ludys if we became separated. My mind plays all sorts of tricks with me. It shows me all the things that might have gone wrong.*

I should have asked Kor more about what he saw. He told me they were no longer with Borssa. I should have asked him where they went. If I hadn't just assumed they would meet me here, I would have. I wonder where they could have gone. What could have happened to them?

Uncle Mitkas tries his best to reassure me but since he has his own bad news to deal with, there's not much he can do. What Kor started at Dragon's Nest has opened the plains up to the Outlanders. Uncle Mitkas sent men as soon as I told him what had happened but they arrived too late to prevent any breach of the barrier.

There are Outlanders now in the plains.

How strange it is to write that.

Such a thing has not happened in as long as anyone can remember. Such a thing has not happened even in our history - at least, as far back as our written history goes. Uncle Mitkas is forming hunting parties to track down the Outlanders that have slipped inside. He says we don't owe that to the plains' people but it ensures our own safety and is therefore worth doing.

That news does little to ease my mind regarding Mother and Otho. Perhaps they are wandering the plains, chased by some of the Outlanders Kor let in. Or perhaps they have already been caught by the Outlanders.

I must stop. I can't keep thinking of all the worst possibilities.

If only Kor had come with me here, I could have asked him to walk their time and find them. But then, I'm not sure I would have been brave enough to learn the truth if it was a bad truth. It's been terrible enough bearing the weight of Father's death. Uncle Mitkas and Jahniss and Naleiah have done everything in their power to console and comfort me but none of it is enough to make up for the gaping hole his absence leaves behind.

It's because I have too much time to think. There's nothing for me to do but attend Uncle Mitkas' court or any one of the frequent parties my cousins either throw themselves or attend with their friends. How I used to miss those when we were wandering the plains! Now they cannot seem to excite me at all.

I'm going to ask Uncle Mitkas today if he will allow me to join the parties hunting down the rogue Outlanders. He's using other trackers for the task so I know he can use me. I need something to do while I wait for word of Mother and Otho and since I had a hand in what happened at Dragon's Nest, it's only right that I help fix it.

Chapter 8

I WAS OFF THE BED AND AT THE open window before anyone could say another word, peering through the darkness at the wall and its watchtowers. The bandage Balia had started wrapping about my hand hung half unraveled as I braced my hands on the windowsill and leaned out, trying to see through the darkness. Somewhere out there, Jarris was waiting for his chance to see the creature.

"You know, perhaps now would be a good time for you to back up your claim," Semptius said in my ear. He stood directly behind my shoulder, his gaze as drawn to the wall of Abirell as mine was. "If you wanted to, that is."

"How?" I twisted around to look at him. There was none of the hunger in his eyes that Brym always had when she demanded I walk time for her.

"Look into the future and tell me what happens to this Outlander. You know, details. Who kills it? How they kill it."

I sighed, sagging against the window frame, and stared back out at the darkness. He wanted me to walk time. My jaw clenched up as I considered his request and weighed it against the promise I'd made myself. The promise I'd already broken once.

He didn't demand the way Brym had. He didn't threaten. He had no tether bound to me to compel my cooperation. I wondered what he would do if I refused. But I have to admit I was too afraid of that possibility to dare deny him.

Shutting my eyes, I drew up the memory of Jarris and I's last conversation. It was easy, although still very painful, to slip into the stream of time. I'd learned its flow. The weeks spent doing it in Dragon's Nest had worn away my body's inhibitions and the pain that filled my head afterwards was no longer the deterrent it had been after the first time.

I still hated that pain.

I hated it more that my body had simply come to accept it.

My sight followed Jarris as he shut the door behind him. Orle had been waiting outside for him, listening into our conversation apparently. Jarris followed the captain down the hallway, down the stairs and out into the night, pausing just long enough for Orle to slip into what I could only imagine was Semptius' room. No doubt that was when he informed Semptius of the conversation between Jarris and I that he'd overheard.

There was no mistaking the anticipation in Jarris' every move. Each step he took was full of barely restrained excitement as he approached his chance to face the thing that had hunted us for so many nights. Nothing made him happier.

Torches lined the palisade and watchtowers, making the scene as visible to my sight as daylight would have. Men moved back and forth on the narrow wooden planks that connected one watchtower to the next. My sight followed Jarris as he ascended the ladder and took his place near Orle on the watchtower to the right of the city gate.

It was sometime before I saw the bell in the watchtower ringing its alarm. No sound came to me with my sight. Jarris was leaning over the wall, intent on whatever creature moved in the darkness.

"Time walker."

I heard Brym's voice in my head even as I was lost to the future. A voice no one else could hear. It startled me, almost enough to send me back into the present. I watched as Orle put an arrow, its tip burning with a blue flame, to his bow and drew the string back. There were men shouting, or at least I thought they were shouting, and pointing. I watched the entire scene play out in eerie silence. The arrow was loosed. Speeding on its way like a shooting star across the night sky, a trail of blue sparks sailing behind it.

It found its target in a flash of incandescent blue and orange.

"Captain Orle kills it with a burning arrow," I said, when I'd pulled myself back into the present.

I was no longer standing at the window, but sitting beneath it, my back to the wall. Outside, the bell was still echoing, each sound a bit quieter than the one before. I leaned my head back against the wall and shut my eyes with a grimace as the ache in my head, no longer held at bay by the future, rushed over me.

"You collapsed. Is that normal?"

Cracking one eye open, I saw that Semptius was now sitting on the bed, his legs crossed underneath him making him look like an overgrown child as he watched me with a perplexed shadow darkening the expression on his face. One of the books was open on his lap and I wondered if he'd been comparing my behavior to that of a past oracle. I wondered if I measured up.

"I guess so." I shut my eyes again and for several minutes Semptius left me to myself, his head bent over the book on his lap.

Footsteps came running down the hall before Semptius spoke again and the door was thrown open a moment later.

Jarris stood framed inside the open doorway, breathing hard but his eyes alight with success and wonder. He froze, taking in Semptius and Balia sitting on the bed and me sitting underneath the window behind them, and the light faded from his eyes at once. His entire face hardened, and one hand dropped to the nearest knife.

"Are you alright, Korris?"

"Is it dead?" Semptius asked, turning to face Jarris, and not giving me a chance to answer.

Jarris gave him a curt nod but kept his eyes on me. I tried to manage a smile and a careless shrug, but my head was throbbing too badly for me to be successful. In fact, my efforts made it worse, and Jarris stalked into the room, his hand sliding his knife partway out of its sheath. Semptius didn't seem to notice but I shook my head, hoping Jarris would understand. Hoping to make him stop before he made things worse.

"And who killed it?"

"I did," Captain Orle said, coming in just then behind Jarris. "Just outside the gates."

Semptius turned to me, and his crooked smile came back. "Well, it seems you either made a very fortunate guess or you truly are the oracle."

"What creature was it?" I asked, pushing myself up a little so the worry would leave Jarris' eyes.

"One that carried plague with it," Orle said. "We haven't seen one of those in years and never inside the barrier. It's completely burned to ash now, though."

I went cold with horror first. Then relief washed through me.

Rensi was wrong.

I wasn't Fentra's curse.

Even though I hadn't allowed myself to believe her words, I couldn't deny how deep they dug their claws into me. But she was wrong. I'd had a part in stopping Brym's attempt to end the world. Maybe coming to Abirell was the right thing to do and maybe I was wrong to fight Jarris so hard on it.

"It's over then," I whispered to myself.

"What's over?"

"Brym...,"

"Old Brym from Dragon's Nest?" Semptius asked. "The one who cannot die?"

"Yes, except she is dead. I killed her." He started at that, only briefly before catching himself, but I didn't miss it. Nor did I miss Captain Orle's raised eyebrows at my statement. "She sent that creature, I think. She meant to wipe out all of the gateways and end the world." I remained silent about my own involvement in her plan.

"Then we are in your debt," Semptius said.

The words cut deep. I hung my head, gripping it between my hands so that they would guess it was only pain that made me hide my face.

"Then perhaps in payment, you will allow my brother and I to leave in peace," Jarris said.

"You are not prisoners here," Semptius said, his one-sided smile returning. "You are free to come and go as you please, although surely waiting for morning would be the wiser choice. And I will readily admit to my own curiosity about Korris and wish to satiate it. Perhaps I can convince you to enjoy our hospitality for a few days. There is much I wish to learn from our new oracle and I think you will find Abirell a welcoming place."

Jarris opened his mouth to answer, looked past Semptius to me, and shut it again. For a moment, he was torn. Then, reaching a decision, he said, "It's up to Korris. If he wishes to stay, we will. But if he wishes to leave..."

"Then you will leave. I understand. And I will not hinder you."

I wished I could believe him.

~   ~   ~

Tormenting agony in my head woke me many hours later.

The room was empty. Only the pile of books still sprawled across one half of the bed remaining to remind me of the previous night's events. Jarris, who'd declared the bed too soft to sleep on and chose the floor instead, was nowhere to be seen.

Pale gray light shone through the cracks of the slatted wooden shutters. Outside, the early morning air was full of bird song and the clatter of cart wheels and the voices of people just beginning their day. The sound of waves breaking against rocks filtered through the rest of the noise and I remembered how close we were to the sea. The sea I'd never seen before.

Clutching my head in my hands, I swung my legs over the side of the bed and stood. It took only a moment of swaying before my balance returned and I could make my way to the window. Throwing open the shutters, I filled my lungs with a full, deep breath of sea freshened air. The sea was somewhere behind me, invisible from the window, but its sound was soothing, and I wondered how I'd missed it the night before.

Below me in the street, peddlers rolled their hand carts along, carrying their merchandise from one end of the city to the other in the hopes of finding willing buyers. I watched them, fascinated, for several minutes. Although there were those among the plains people that peddled wares and services, it was done in a very different manner.

When two tribes met, either through intention or by accident, those with things to sell would meet in the space between. They would spread out their large horse skin blankets on the ground and arrange their merchandise upon that. Stories, news, and meals would be shared between the two tribes and often the chieftains of both would sit together at a single large fire directly between the two. Those gatherings were often the highlight of our summer wanderings.

With an almost irrepressible urge, I found myself longing to wander the streets of Abirell; to walk to the edge of the sea and put my hand in it; to mingle with those people who lived so differently from anything I'd ever seen. My longing to return to the rest of my family was tempered slightly by my longing to see Abirell.

I leaned out the window, my eyes taking in just as much as they could of the wooden city.

Hunger made me look around to see if any of the meal Balia had brought the night before remained. Not even the tray was left behind, which was a bit startling since I couldn't remember waking to her being in the room. The woman moved so silently. I'd yet to hear her speak.

It was that same hunger that led me out the door and into the hallway. I'd half feared to find it locked or guarded on the other side but Semptius either meant what he'd said or was more subtle about forcing us to stay. The hallway was deserted, and I stood for a moment or two trying to decide where I should go to find both Jarris and food.

Going back down the stairs I'd come up the night before seemed like a reasonable plan and from there the aroma of food guided me.

Chapter 9

SEMPTIUS GLANCED UP FROM the stack of books he was buried behind. I recognized most of them as having been tossed on my bed the night before. He must have retrieved them while I ate a rather large and satisfying breakfast of sweet breads, mutton and fruit. Captain Orle had found me at breakfast and asked on Semptius' behalf if I would consider spending at least one morning with the governor to answer his questions.

The room I found myself in was small but not in a way that felt cramped or stifled. Two walls were lined with wooden shelves overflowing with books and papers, some of them looking ancient enough to have existed since the days of dragons. They made the room smell a little musty. A third wall was almost entirely taken up by a great stone hearth, inside of which was a rather weak and feeble fire.

A small round table, which Semptius was sitting behind, and two chairs made up the only furniture in the room. It was toward the back of the great house, tucked away so that its occupants were undisturbed by the coming and going of anyone else.

I stood, my back pressed against the door, my hand resting on the latch, ready to run if Semptius made any move toward me. The knowledge that Jarris waited just outside the door was comforting even if Jarris alone couldn't stop Semptius from keeping me if he chose.

Even after Semptius' assurances the night before, I didn't dare believe his seemingly innocent intentions. No one who knew what I was let me go so easily.

"You are not very trusting, are you?" Semptius asked, his face wrinkled up in bemusement at my obvious wariness. "Do you see a chain around here?"

Sparing the small room a quick glance, I shook my head but only moved forward a step. The only reason I'd agreed to meet Semptius was because I was curious. About the books and what they said and what Semptius might add to my slowly growing store of knowledge about my own gift.

And because Jarris was desperate to stay long enough to get his hands on firedust. It had been all he spoke of at breakfast. Apparently, the sight of it burning the Outlander to ash had been spectacular. I couldn't stomach the thought of seeing it up close, not after Dragon's Nest and how close I'd come to dying in that inferno.

"And I couldn't tether you even if I wanted to."

"Your periapt isn't strong enough?" I made no effort to keep the doubt from my voice. I'd never heard of a periapt that couldn't tether. That was their most fundamental purpose.

Semptius laughed, the sound of it deeper than his voice and surprising. It was the sort of laugh that made you want to laugh in turn. "No, Korris. I cannot tether you because I have no periapt."

"But you are..."

"The governor of Abirell, yes. We used to have a king. The periapt was his."

Semptius rose from his seat and went to one of the shelves. He reached for an object I hadn't noticed before; a vial of glass, the liquid inside the same color as the blood I'd seen spilled on the white snow beneath the mountains in the north.

"He and the queen both died the same night under most tragic circumstances and their infant child was stolen from his crib only to be found abandoned and dead just outside our borders many hours later. They left no other blood heir and so this, the king's periapt of dragon's blood, has become utterly useless to any of us. And, to be honest, I think we're better off without it anyway."

Curiosity carried me across the room, and I sat down in the second chair, facing him, and held out my hand. He dropped the vial onto my waiting palm, and I held it up to the firelight. A faint glow surrounded the vial, evidence of the power contained within.

Power that was trapped forever without a blood heir.

My free hand felt for Brym's eye of a dragon periapt that hung still about my neck, a keepsake of my newfound freedom. No such glow came from it, convincing me once and for all that it was not so great a periapt as she thought it was.

"How do you rule without it?" I'd never heard of such a thing. Even the smallest, most insignificant tribe was ruled by a chieftain who carried one.

"As difficult as it is to believe, Korris, the periapts aren't necessary for ruling. I think, if you'll give yourself a chance to see it, that you'll find Abirell quite a happy and thriving city without one."

"What is it you wanted from me?" I asked as I continued to gaze, mesmerized, at the light filtering through the blood. It turned the light red as it spilled out on the other side.

"Did you know oracles of the past were always the firstborn children of kings?"

"I've heard it once or twice." From Borssa and then from Brym.

"Yes, it led to an odd tradition when it came to the line of succession. According to our histories, no one trusted oracles as kings and so thrones were passed to the second born. Foresight was the only gift ever limited in such a manner. You seem to be an exception to that, though." Semptius glanced up at me and smiled pleasantly. "You haven't mentioned who your father is."

I stiffened at his words, at the probing of them.

Not quite a question.

But most definitely seeking an answer.

Drakkus had wanted to know who my father was. Brym had wanted to know who my father was. Now Semptius wanted to know who my father was. The pattern was disconcerting.

Semptius had worn my guard down with his easy and friendly manner. It returned with his last words. He was like everyone else, even when he protested the fact. I was just a gift to him, just a thing to take apart and figure out and use. He seemed most interested in the taking apart and figuring out.

"He's just a chieftain of the plains." Although Brym had insisted, quite vehemently and confidently, that he wasn't.

"Ah. Perhaps the Fates have decided to change the rules by which they give gifts. They are rather fond of playing games with us poor mortals."

The Fates and their games. I thought back to the strange woman who'd been part dream, part reality. Destiny, she'd called herself. Destiny, who didn't like others tampering with her game pieces. Destiny, who had claimed that whatever game was being played was already well begun and could not be changed.

I turned the vial over in my hand, watching the liquid shift.

Semptius had returned to his book, his head bent over the pages. He flipped from one to the next and then back again, switching between pages and books so fast that I didn't see how it was possible he could actually be reading anything from them at all.

"Do you have any books that speak of Fentra?"

"Fentra. Fentra." Semptius tapped the book in front of him at that moment with one finger and squinted up at the bookshelf. "Fentra the madwoman. Fentra the cursed. Fentra the last of her kind. She went by many names, that woman did. Yes, we have writings of her. To be honest, Korris, they are among my least favorite to read. Such a sad woman and such a sad end."

"She was murdered."

His face pinched into a quick frown, and he turned his head away from me. "Executed. At least, depending on the account. And there are many accounts."

"Why?"

Semptius rose and began his restless pacing, his hands clasped together behind his back as if he meant to lecture me. "That is the question, isn't it? And I thought I was the one who wanted to ask all the questions."

"Why?" I repeated. I'd asked it before, but no one had given me an answer. I wanted an answer now.

"Because she had gone mad with the burden of her gift. Or because she'd foretold a future no one wanted to hear and angered them. Or because others were afraid of her and what she could do. The reasons are endless, and no one now knows which one is the correct one." He turned to me, a sadness in his eyes that I had not seen before. "You are right, I suppose, to fear me and to fear others. You are different and the world is not kind to things that are different. And I think you have already felt that unkindness."

"Will you keep me here against my will?"

"I have told you already that I will not."

There was a time when I'd believed Drakkus when it made no sense to. I'd believed him because something inside me knew he spoke the truth. In that moment, I knew Semptius spoke the truth as well and I believed him. And with that belief came a sense of relief so strong, so free that I felt I could fly upon it.

"Then you are different, too. Has the world been unkind to you?"

Semptius gave me another sad smile. "Not in the same way that you have experienced. But enough about me. What you did last night, when you looked into the future, how did you do that? What is it like when you are in the future? Are you still aware of the present?" Questions spilled out of him, and he stopped, catching himself. "Forgive me. I've spent my whole life reading about the past and its oracles. I simply never thought I'd live to see the day when the Silence was broken and an oracle walked among men once more."

As if I were still not quite human in his eyes. "It's hard to explain."

But explain it, I did. As best I could, at least. More than once, Semptius held up a finger to halt my explanation and read from one of the many books he kept flipping through - comparing my words against stories of past oracles, I assumed.

The morning passed before I knew it, taking with it the last of my fears. Semptius sifted through the pages of at least a dozen books, pulling ideas and questions from each, his need for answers as insatiable as a fire's need for fuel.

CHAPTER 10

I N MY HAND I HELD A handful of coins such as I'd never possessed in my life. Semptius had given them to me, insisting that they were nothing more than a gift. I stepped into the room Jarris and I had shared the night before but found it empty. Jarris had disappeared as soon as our midday meal was complete, and I had assumed he'd returned to our room.

I was wrong.

No doubt he was off, possibly with Captain Orle, still trying to get his hands on firedust before we left the next morning.

For a moment, I debated - torn between staying in the room where I knew he would come find me again and taking to the streets of Abirell to explore the city that was ruled by choice and not periapt. Months before, the decision would have been simple. I wouldn't have dreamed of going off alone. But that was before I'd spent weeks traversing the harsh plains alone. That was before I'd navigated Brym's world on my own.

My mind hovered between the two choices only briefly before my feet carried me back down the stairs and out the front door of the governor's house. Out into the exotic world of Abirell.

Outside, the sun was high and the sky clear. The air was fresh with seawater and spring. And I was free of any tether or chain or bargain that involved other lives. Even the weight of guilt that had accompanied me from Dragon's Nest was gone - destroyed just as the plague Outlander had been destroyed.

For once, Rensi's parting words didn't hover over every thought in my mind. I wondered briefly if she had made it back to Ludys and if she still thought as badly of me as she had when we parted ways. But those thoughts were too dismal to share the same space as my happier ones, so I dismissed them quickly.

The bustle of the streets was almost as intoxicating as the incense Borssa had burned on that mountain top the night he and Drakkus tried to steal my gift. The noise, the people, the colors, the sounds; all worked their way inside my head, loosening the months old tension that I'd grown accustomed to, and my steps were lighter for it. I wandered down the wide road Orle had led us in on. Past the governor's house and toward the beckoning sound of the sea.

People wandered in and out of shops that lined the road. I tried to guess what each shop sold by the parcels that were carried out since I couldn't read any of their signs. There was a shop that displayed loaves of bread, all shapes and sizes, in their front window. Another sold woven cloth, the door propped open enough for me to see a man and a woman both busy at their own giant looms. There was a shop that sold meat, with carcasses hanging along the back wall.

Along the road, peddlers set up their carts and wares and called out to those who passed them, urging buyers to pay attention. Jewelry, bright skeins of thread, charms, leather wares. All those and more competed for buyers on the busy streets.

It was hard to recall how hushed and still the streets had been just the night before. I wondered if they always retired so early or if perhaps the rumors of Outlanders reaching the plains had instilled a sense of caution in them. That caution had disappeared with the rising sun.

A group of children, dressed only to the waist like most of the men, scampered through the streets in wild games of chase. I stopped, watching them and thinking of a time not so long ago when I would have gladly joined in such a game. My little sister, Ahashi, still would.

Semptius had claimed that Abirell was better off without the use of a periapt. What I saw on the streets began to convince me that his words were true. Even amongst the tribes, I'd never seen so many happy, carefree people. They smiled in greeting when they met my eyes. They laughed often, the sound of it more foreign than I'd thought it would be. I'd had so little room for laughter in months. The bits and pieces of their conversations that I heard were good natured.

Abirell was truly a place of wonder, and I was falling in love with it. No one around me knew who I was or what gift was mine.

Their ignorance was my freedom.

A freedom I had not tasted once in my life. I'd always been different, always been on the outside looking in, even inside the tribe where I belonged. But there, on the streets of Abirell, I was just another person, another part of the crowd.

My eyes were so busy, darting from one new scene to the next, that I missed seeing the woman as she rounded the corner in front of me. We collided. The coins in my hand and the basket full of spring herbs in her hand scattered everywhere in a rain of green and bronze.

Startled, I stooped down to retrieve the fallen items, murmuring an apology. As I reached out my hand to pick up the scattered coins, I noticed that the bandage Balia had tied around my old scar was soaked with blood. I wanted to be annoyed with it, but the mood of the city had worked its way inside of me and I shrugged the annoyance off, not willing for it to ruin the best day of my life in the past several months.

At least, I shrugged it off until I glanced up and caught sight of a face that made the hairs on my neck rise and my chest tighten.

Muttering another apology, I snatched up the last of my fallen coins, no longer thinking of what I should spend them on nor how much I wanted to see the sea and dip my hand into it. Only thinking of a cold night, high up on a mountain, with blood flowing freely from the palm of my hand, mingling with another's.

All the warmth of the sun was snatched away from me then as if a great cloud had moved over it. And yet the sun shone as brightly as ever.

All the good-natured merriment of those I shared the street with disappeared, lost in a sinister wave of doubt. And yet, when I looked about me, nothing had changed. The townspeople about me still gossiped and bartered and chatted in the same agreeable way.

My hand was bleeding.

My hand had been bleeding since we neared Abirell.

And now I was pretty sure I knew the reason.

My footsteps were heavy with dread, all the lightness from before gone out of them, as I slipped in and out of the throngs of people on the street, following the retreating figure of Otho.

He left the main street with its shops and multitudes of people and turned down one of the narrow roads that were lined with houses. It would have been impossible to stay out of sight if he'd had any suspicion that he was being followed. Since he didn't turn his head once, I don't think the thought ever crossed his mind.

Another turn. Another street. Another row of wooden houses with wooden boxes hanging beneath each window; each box full of bright, spring flowers every shade of pink and purple and orange and yellow and red. He stopped in front of one house whose flowers were less vibrant and tended to, their petals and leaves drooping with neglect, and lifted his hand to the latch on the door.

It was only then that I noticed his own hand bound up in a bandage that was stained red with blood. I wondered if his scar hurt as it bled or if it felt the same warm pulse that mine did.

I waited until he was inside and then approached the house. Otho had not shut the door fully behind him and I stood there at the entrance, listening, waiting for someone to speak. I was not kept waiting long.

"It's still bleeding," Otho said, his voice muffled by the door between us.

"What did he say?" Rayka said.

"He tried to heal it again, but he said it was already healed and there was nothing more he could do. You don't think he could guess what it came from, do you?"

Rayka's response was too quiet for me to catch.

"There're rumors, you know. Everybody's talking about an Outlander in the plains. Apparently, it came up to the city gate before it was killed," Otho said. "You don't think it's begun, do you?"

What madness overcame me then, to open a door that I would have been better off leaving shut, I'd never know.

I never wanted to see either of them again, but a million questions floated through my head and my hand was shoving the door aside before my mind had caught up with itself. It made no sound as it opened, its hinges too well oiled. I stood there, just inside the threshold and stared at the room that smelled of herbs and medicines and blood.

And stared.

Otho was crouching in front of a fire, his side to me, stirring it to renewed life with an iron poker. He had but to turn his head a little and I would be caught. Rayka's back was to me, leaning over a form lying on a bed.

Drakkus.

She was leaning over Drakkus, a cup in her hand, lifting his head to help him drink.

I just stared.

I'd seen him die. I was so sure I'd seen him die.

And why were they here? Why had they not returned to Ludys, like Rensi said they would?

The moment of stunned disbelief came to a jarring end when Otho turned a little and saw me, his eyes widening and his face paling. His gaze darted from me to his bleeding hand and then back to me.

"Kor?" he said in a soft whisper, one that didn't reach his mother's ears. He glanced from her to me and back at her and shook his head a little as if to chase me away.

A voice in my head told me to retreat, to close the door behind me and never look back again.

I ignored it.

I stood there, knowing that only a few seconds separated me from Rayka's discovery of my presence. I stood there, feeling as if the entire world had stilled and time stopped. I knew that Rayka would turn, that she would see me, that once she did there would be no quick escape for me. She would speak. She'd ask me questions I didn't want to answer and offer apologies I wasn't interested in hearing. Yet, still, I stood there.

"Korris?" Rayka's gasp broke the stillness as she turned and caught sight of me. Her eyes widened just as Otho's had and then drifted past me, to the empty street out the door. Hopeful. Longing. Searching. "Where's Rensi? Is she with you? Is she alright?"

I couldn't answer right away. I forgot, for a moment, to breathe and then, when I remembered, it was too hard and too fast.

The last time I'd seen Otho in person, I'd been kneeling, naked and cold and bleeding, on a rock facing him. He'd been equally naked and cold and bleeding, his hand pinned beneath mine by Borssa's knife. Memories of that night flooded my mind. Everything about it had been so wrong and so far beyond my control. I looked at Otho, wondering if the same memories assaulted him, but he wouldn't meet my eyes.

They'd been trying to take my gift. Stealing it from me. Taking what was mine. The violation of that night rolled over me and my heart stuttered, and my chest tightened until all I saw was Otho's blanched face as I knelt there that night and all I heard was Borssa's raspy voice droning on about fates and firstborns and kings and nonsense that didn't matter when they were robbing me of a part of myself.

"I left her," I said, not thinking of how the words would sound. Not thinking of how harsh and callous they were as they broke the silence.

Rayka's face fell, and she turned away, allowing me my first real look at Drakkus.

He lay unmoving on the bed, his eyes shut, his skin an awful gray. His chest rose and fell, though, with the rhythm of breathing and I knew that somehow I'd been mistaken in my vision. That Jarris was right, and the tether had continued to work because its holder still lived.

And I wasn't sure if it was relief I felt at that or anger. I wasn't sure if I'd hoped all along that he had survived or if I'd truly been thankful for his death. All I knew was that seeing him alive still awoke some feeling in me, even if I didn't know what it was.

My hand went to my wrist, fingering the space where that tether had sat for months, robbing me of freedom, binding me to people I hated.

I'd been better off not knowing. Better off letting the memory of that night slip into the recesses of my mind where it was neglected. Better off forgetting – if such a thing were possible.

Without another word, I turned and fled.

~   ~   ~

Seagulls swooped and dove above my head, their calls new and haunting in my ears. Along the sandy stretch of shoreline, the men and women who made their livelihood off the sea worked.

I'd never seen the big wooden boats that bobbed in the silvery water. On the largest of them, great canvas sheets were held aloft by an upright beam. The same wind that swept the plains grass into rippling waves of green caught inside the sails of the boats and drove them forward.

The pebble I'd plucked out of the sand sailed through the air in a satisfying arc before disappearing with a splash beneath the surface of the water, sending ripples across the waves.

I had almost returned to the governor's house after leaving Rayka and Drakkus and Otho. It was only my longing to see the sea at least once before Jarris and I left the following morning that turned my steps towards the endless expanse of water. That, and I wasn't ready to talk to anyone just then. I needed the space to think, to put everything back together that my discovery had torn apart.

The sea, every shade of silver and green that I could imagine, was more magnificent than I could have dreamed, stretching on and on until it met the sky in a thin dark line on the distant horizon. On either side of it, heavily wooded mountains rose up, framing the sea inside their mighty, jagged outlines. I'm not sure what I would have seen if I could have looked around those mountains - if it would have been more water or if the water gave way to the Outlands.

As I watched an especially large boat loose its sail and catch the wind, I tried to imagine the feel of that wind on my face and the spray of the waves on my skin.

I wanted to sail, and I hadn't known it until that moment.

Probably just as badly as Jarris wanted his firedust.

"Where does it go?" I asked an old man who sat near me, his hands busy with a net.

He looked over at me, his weathered face all wrinkles and sunspots. "Where does what go?"

"The sea. When you go past the horizon, what's there?"

He turned to stare out at it, a hand shielding his eyes from the sunlight reflected off the water. "More sea. Though some say there's land somewhere in the beyond. We don't sail that far."

"Why not?" I couldn't imagine turning my back on that beckoning horizon and leaving it behind. If I was on a ship, I was sure I would keep going until I found the place where the sky and sea met.

"Sea demons," the old man said, spitting after he said the last word.

Sea demons. Outlanders. We were surrounded by monsters, trapped in our little world with no escape even as our world hurtled towards its doom. I left the old man to his net mending and wandered a bit further down the sandy stretch of beach, tossing in pebbles as I went.

My thoughts were interrupted by the intrusion of Otho's voice as he said, "There's something you should know."

Spinning around and taking an instinctive step back from him, I said nothing, only stared at him. He'd grown a bit taller over the winter, his shoulders had grown a bit broader. He'd be every bit as big as his father when he was finished growing, a thought that gave me a little twist of envy. And his health had apparently returned after that long night on the mountain top. He stood there, thrusting his hands into his pockets like he was angry at them for being attached to him, gazing at anything and everything except me.

"The ritual didn't work," he finally blurted out, still not meeting my eyes.

"You followed me here just to say that? I already knew that."

"At least, it didn't work the way Father thought it would. It didn't give me your gift."

He paused and I waited as he pulled his hands free of his pockets and picked at an invisible speck on his sleeve. Whatever it was he wanted to tell me wasn't coming easily and dread filled my heart.

"I know that, too. I still get the visions."

"You do. And so do I. Sort of. But I don't think they're mine. They don't feel like mine."

"What?"

He stepped past me so that his back was to me and stared out at the sea. "Did you foresee Mother and I running away from Borssa?"

"Yes."

"And you foresaw a lot of that old woman's time?"

"Brym? Yes." I bent to pick up another pebble, rolling it around between my fingers to distract myself. I tossed Otho's questions around in my head, searching for their purpose and finding nothing but confusion. What was more confusing than his questions was why I was still standing there talking to him and not fleeing back to the governor's house.

"You saw into Ren's future a bit, too, didn't you?" Otho's voice caught a little over his sister's name.

"Yes," I said for the third time, shuddering a little as I remembered just what it was that I'd seen in Rensi's time. "But how do you know about all of that?"

Otho let out a heavy breath and his hands returned to his pockets. He kicked at the sand and dug the toe of his boot into the stuff. "I was afraid none of that was just bad dreams."

"What are you talking about?"

"I didn't take your gift from you. I still can't foresee anything on my own. But every time you see into the future, I see it too. That night when Borssa... after he put the knife in... it all just came at once. I think it must have been every vision you've ever had. It was..."

When his voice trailed off, unable to say anymore, I tried to count up in my head all the visions I'd had up to that point. I gave up when I remembered how often I saw the world ending when I was ill.

Awful. That's what it would have been.

No wonder Otho had been so much worse off than I after that ritual. It was a wonder he'd recovered at all.

His words sent a sliver of ice through me, and I swallowed hard. My fingers curled around the pebble I'd taken up, pressing the sharp edges of it deep into the palm of my hand. Otho shared something of mine, something I'd never willingly given him. He shared a part of my mind in a way I hadn't even imagined possible.

I sank within myself, searching for the anger and hate I knew I would find. Searching for it because I needed it. I needed something to hold onto that I could trust. But instead, I came up empty handed.

No.

Worse than empty handed. I came up feeling sorry for Otho, feeling bad that he was now burdened with the weight of my visions as well. I recoiled, confused. It was as if all my anger at him had evaporated into nothingness and that made no sense.

Glancing up at Otho, his eyes darted away from mine. "I know," was all he said.

"What did you do to me?" I asked, but even those words carried none of the fury I wanted them to. They sounded mild, curious, nothing more. As if I didn't really care that Otho was now an unwelcome witness to all my sight. As if he hadn't been part of a violation that I would never forget.

Otho winced, not at my anger but at my indifference. "I don't really know but I think... I think, maybe, that Borssa... I think he might have made a blood bond between us."

CHAPTER 11

*I*T'S A DREADFUL BUSINESS, REN."

That's what Uncle Mitkas says every single day when the couriers bring him news. They are coming and going constantly, these couriers. And with each missive they bring, Uncle Mitkas grows a little more silent, a little more withdrawn. There's trouble everywhere, it seems, and as he says, it is dreadful business.

Just today, at lunch, a courier arrived. Uncle Mitkas used to make them wait until he was finished with his meal, but he abandoned that practice after the first of his men reached Dragon's Nest and sent their report back. Today's news came from Dragon's Nest. Uncle Mitkas just frowned deeper and deeper as he read it. He wouldn't say what news it contained but he turned to me and asked me, "Do you know why the Outlanders never cross the mountains and can only come through the gateways, Ren?"

I told him I didn't. To be honest, I never gave it much thought. It's just something that's always been until Kor set Edronn and the others to burning down Dragon's Nest. The mountains protected us from the Outlands. I've never given much thought as to why.

"Because those mountains have veins of firedust running through them. More firedust than you can imagine. The Outlanders know it," he said to me. "They smell the stuff. They don't dare cross them with so much firedust inside them. Do you know what happened when that oracle convinced your father's men to set a fire inside the mountain?"

I did know. As soon as he explained to me, I knew. It wasn't just the firedust scattered on the floor that burned, it was the firedust trapped inside the mountain itself.

"They didn't just bring down half of Dragon's Nest, they widened the gateway. I'll have to send more soldiers if it's to be contained."

He didn't say another word to anyone for the rest of the meal and even Jahniss and Naleiah have been somber ever since. It really was such dreadful news to receive.

When I'm sitting here alone, with nothing but the crickets and night birds to keep my thoughts company, it's easy to think of dreadful things. I wonder if Kor knew what would happen when Edronn set the first fire. He had a vision before and he said he'd walked time to find another way. I wonder if he knew, like he did of the attack on our camp, and chose not to tell anyone. He might have. If he thought Dragon's Nest deserved it and I'm sure he thought that. Just like he thought Father deserved to die in that attack.

I'm still trying hard not to hate Kor for that.

There, you see. My thoughts turn very dark when left to wander about on their own. Perhaps they would be less dark if I had more pleasant things to think on. Instead, they turn to worrying over Mother and Otho's continued absence. Uncle Mitkas has instructed every party he's sent out hunting Outlanders to keep their eyes open for any sign of Mother and Otho. So far, none have heard so much as whisper about them. When I think of what that might mean, when I think of how empty my life will be without any of them, I want to lie down and sob and never get up again.

"Despair doesn't solve any problems."

That's what Naloni says. It is a comfort to find her here still after everything that happened between Father and Uncle Mitkas. I was so afraid to come back and find no one I knew but Uncle Mitkas kept most of the old staff on.

Anyway, I think Naloni is right. Despair isn't going to fix this. Perhaps nothing will. Perhaps Father was right and we are living through the end of our world. There's some old prophecy or lore about that. If that is true, then I need to face the end doing something.

Uncle Mitkas has only reluctantly agreed to allow me to join the next hunting party he sends out and only after I resorted to begging. They'll be leaving in just a few days. I don't know if I'm more excited to finally have something to do other than sit and worry or if I'm more terrified of seeing another Outlander. The caged ones were bad enough.

Chapter 12

I MISSED SEEING JARRIS WAITING just outside the front door of the governor's house as I hurried toward it, my head bowed, and my arms wrapped around myself in a vain effort to hold myself together. I was unaware of my brother's presence until his hands landed on my shoulders, halting my half jogging steps.

"Where have you been?"

Instinct made me pull away from him, startled. I lifted my chin, meeting his eyes. And although I knew that he was only worried, I shoved him away from me. Whatever Borssa and Drakkus had done to me that night on the mountaintop had prevented me from being angry with Otho. There was nothing to prevent me from being angry at anyone else.

Jarris, unfortunately, was the one in front of me.

"Where have *you* been?" I snapped back at him.

"I was with Orle, like I told you I would be."

I shrugged his hands off and started past him, but Jarris' hand darted out and caught me by the shoulder, stopping me in my tracks once more.

"You've been gone for hours, though, and you didn't tell anyone. Where have you been? You know it's not safe for you to just wander around on your own. Not after everything that's happened. Someone could have snatched you away again."

I knew I shouldn't have but I laughed. I laughed because almost every time I had been snatched away it had been when I was surrounded by people who were supposed to look out for me. In fact, the only exception was the attack by Brym's men.

"You're forgetting that I've managed the last several weeks just fine on my own, Jarris. I crossed the plains on my own. And since when have you ever stopped someone from taking me when they wanted to? Not once. That's how many times. Not once out of five different times."

Jarris was speechless. A strange look flitted across his face, one I couldn't decipher. His mouth opened, but no words came out. He let me go when I tried to slip past him again. I didn't look back.

Not even the smell of the evening meal could quench the rage that boiled, restless and hungry, inside of me. I bypassed the dining hall and went straight up the stairs and into the room Jarris and I shared, letting the door slam shut with a satisfying crash behind me. Then and only then did the tiniest murmur of guilt push its way into the roar of anger inside my head.

I flung myself onto the bed, leaning my back against the headboard and drawing my knees up to my chest. For some minutes, I did nothing but stare at the bare wall, clinging to an anger that I knew Jarris didn't deserve but that I didn't want to let go of either. I wasn't ready to let go of it. I was right to be angry. I was right to be furious.

Otho was a part of me.

Otho, who had held me in disdain, who had disbelieved my gift, had a part in my gift. No vision would come again without the memory that he shared it with me, whether I wanted him to or not. I wondered if my visions and time walking was all he saw or if he shared my thoughts as well and had just thought better than to say that.

I ground my teeth together trying to force my hatred onto Otho, but it didn't work. It just melted away into understanding and pity or, at the very least, indifference.

The only way I had of knowing that time passed was the sinking sun outside the window. The room dimmed and grew dark, but I didn't bother to get up and light any of the numerous candles that were arrayed around the room. The darkness suited me just fine. A cool, evening breeze, heavy with the smell of the sea and of coming rain and fresh bloomed flowers, blew in through the open shutters, making me shiver a little.

Footsteps came down the hallway and stopped outside the door. I knew before the door opened that it was Jarris and I wished I'd had time to lay down and pretend to be asleep before he entered. That would have been easier than facing his wrath. And I was quite sure that he was angry after what I'd said. Again. In just a few days, I'd managed to earn my oldest brother's ire twice – a feat I had never accomplished before.

Instead, light from the hallway behind him flooded in, revealing me sitting upright on the bed.

Jarris said nothing when he entered. He just moved about the room, lighting a handful of candles. Lowering himself to the floor opposite the bed and leaning back against the wall, he pulled out one of his knives and began the meticulous process of sharpening it. The sound of the thin metal blade screeching against the whetstone was the only sound in the room for a while.

I watched him, like I had watched him at least a thousand times before while sitting around one of our campfires.

There were words I wanted to say that I knew I couldn't get out. I wanted to tell him I was sorry and that I didn't blame him for all the times I was captured by neighboring tribes. The words choked up inside my throat, refusing to be spoken.

The silence grew long. Uncomfortable and uneasy. I unraveled the bandage that Balia had put on my hand and ran my finger over the newly formed scab. It had stopped bleeding. It must have stopped after I'd met Otho. I wondered if it would bleed again or if it that was finished for good. And all the while, the only sound in the room was the whine of metal against whetstone.

"Jarris?"

My brother grunted a response that wasn't really a response without looking up from his task. I sighed. He was definitely still angry.

I chewed on my lip, not sure whether I wanted to go on or not. I didn't want Jarris to stay angry with me. He almost never was. Then again, I'd never yelled at him before like I had just done.

When I didn't say anything else, he finally looked up, his eyes narrowing. "What?" he said.

I looked back down at my hand and thought of the question I'd been about to ask him. "Nothing."

"What?" he demanded.

"Have you ever heard about blood rituals that didn't work out the way they were supposed to?"

"Yours," he said flatly. "We don't do them for a reason. It's only the mountain folk that do."

"But have you ever heard of what can happen when they go wrong?"

Jarris shrugged and with that movement, the last vestiges of his anger disappeared. "Ask Semptius. He seems to know a lot about a lot."

"It's fine. I was just curious."

It took Jarris less than a minute of studying me to decide that my question was rooted in more than idle curiosity. Sheathing his knife, he stood and came to sit on the bed in front of me.

"Let me see your hand."

With a reluctant sigh, I extended my arm and laid my hand in his. His calloused fingers slid over the scar and the now dried blood as he frowned.

Sometimes, I hated how much Jarris saw when he looked at a person. Sometimes, I hated how quickly his mind worked and how little time it took for him to connect a few tidbits of information. He said nothing but I could see from the way his expression hardened that he'd guessed the purpose of my questioning.

I pulled my hand back and tucked it under my other arm. "We're leaving tomorrow, anyway. It doesn't matter."

"Actually..."

"Jarris, you said we would. You said it was up to me and I don't want to stay another day. I want to go home."

"I know but if we leave in the morning then I won't get my knives."

"What knives? You have yours already," I said, gesturing to the one he'd just sheathed at his side.

"Orle told me that blades forged in furnaces that use firedust can kill Outlanders just as well as the firedust can. I want some."

"So, we're not leaving in the morning?" That fact shouldn't have made my gut twist the way it did. It shouldn't have sent fingers of dread crawling up my spine.

"The morning after. They'll be finished tomorrow. There's even one for you. And then we won't have to run from any more Outlanders. We'll be able to make our way back to the Iron Towers without any trouble."

It all made sense. None of it was unreasonable. We would be safer armed with weapons capable of killing an Outlander. We would likely have no trouble reaching the Iron Towers. But none of that quelled the growing uneasiness inside me at the thought of spending another night in Abirell, which made no sense.

Abirell was the friendliest, most welcoming place I'd ever been.

Semptius had been nothing but kind and had made no demands for the use of my gift. I had a freedom in Abirell that I had nowhere else.

Since I had no real reason to tell him no, I said, "As long as I'm getting one of those knives, then I suppose we can stay another night."

~   ~   ~

Morning found me standing once more inside the small, book-filled room that Semptius seemed to love. Instead of buried beneath a pile of books, though, I found him scratching away with quill and ink, his hand moving so quickly that the marks seemed to appear on the parchment like magic.

Semptius barely glanced up long enough to wave me in. I sat down across from him and let several minutes go by in silence as he finished his writing.

Sitting on the table where I'd left it the morning before was the vial of dragon's blood. I picked it up and turned it over in my hands as I waited, admiring the fine cuts on the glass of the vial that made it sparkle red with the sunlight.

"I thought you and your brother meant to be off this morning?" Semptius said as he set aside his quill and ink pot.

"Jarris wanted to wait another day."

"Ah... Captain Orle had mentioned something about him wanting special weapons made. It seems your brother is rather enthralled by the wonders of firedust. It is likely for the best, considering that Outlanders have breached the mountain barrier. You won't always be near enough to a gateway to slip away from them."

I hadn't really come to talk to Semptius about Jarris or his newfound enthusiasm for firedust. I would have been more than happy to never see the black powder again in my life. I'd seen what it could do, the destruction it wreaked. How quickly it could be lost control of. I'd felt its heat breathing down my neck.

"Do you know anything about blood rituals?" I asked without wasting any more time.

Semptius smiled, one side of his mouth twisting up the way it always did and there was a humor in his eyes that told me my question wasn't nearly as unexpected as I had thought it might be. "This question wouldn't have anything to do with your hand, would it?"

"You knew what it was as soon as you saw it, didn't you?" I asked, remembering his interest in it when Balia was bandaging it.

"I must confess, I did. You seemed rather reluctant to discuss it, though. Who performed the ritual on you?"

I turned the dragon's blood vial over and over, watching the crimson liquid inside it. The blood reminded me of that night on the mountain top and of the day Brym's men came. Rather than answer his question, I asked another of my own.

"Do you know what happens when one goes wrong?"

"All sorts of things can happen. Blood rituals have a way of binding people together. Sometimes, they can be a way of transferring one thing to another person. Many years ago, they were used as a marriage pact, although that practice has died out for a number of reasons. The trouble with blood rituals, and the reason they are forbidden in many places, is the fact that they are wildly unpredictable. That, and they have the tendency to be performed on unwilling participants."

His words floated through my head as I stared at the vial of blood. Sunlight shone through the window and onto it. The two combined to make a faint red beam of light.

"What's the worst thing that can happen when one goes wrong?"

"They don't go wrong, as you keep saying. They go however the Fates choose to make them go - which is why they are terribly unpredictable. But I think the worst thing that can happen is binding one life to another. So that if one dies, both die."

My eyes widened and I sucked in a sharp breath. My fingers curled around the glass vial, gripping it hard as the meaning of his words became clear. It was warm, as if it had been lying in the sun. Its warmth was calming, soothing; even if the blood inside reminded me of sights I wished to forget.

All at once, I needed out of that small room. The air was stifling, the walls closing in around me. I wanted, needed space to breathe and to think. Rising from my chair, I thanked him quickly and dashed out the door, heading for the streets and the calming sea.

I was out in the street before I noticed the vial of dragon's blood still in my hand. Sliding it into a pocket, I promised myself I'd return it just as soon as I came back.

CHAPTER 13

I BLAME IT ON THE BLOOD bond that I never arrived at the seashore but instead found myself standing once more in front of a door I knew I ought never to open. It was shut fully, unlike the day before when I'd followed Otho to it. But even so, I could hear the soft murmur of voices, although the words themselves were lost to me.

The latch lifted easily, and the door swung open silently, revealing a scene that wasn't all that different from the day before. Drakkus still lay in the single bed along the back wall of the room. Rayka sat in a chair beside him, her hands busy with something in her lap, her head bent to her work. Otho sat on the floor in front of the fireplace, whittling a sharp point onto the end of a thick stick.

As sunlight flooded in behind me, Rayka and Otho both looked up, startled by my sudden and unannounced entrance.

I stood there, twisting my hands together, not knowing what to say or do or why I'd even come back in the first place. My feet carried me one step into the room, and then another and another until I was halfway between the still open door and Drakkus' bed.

The man who lay in front of me shared few similarities to the man who'd stolen me from my family. His face was thin, gaunt; hollowed out with months of illness. Whatever injuries he'd received at the hands of Brym's men had come close to killing him, of that I was sure as I stared at him. He would have died if Rayka and Otho hadn't run from Borssa when they had.

I took another step closer as Rayka tensed, her hands closing into tight fists around the cloth that she was sewing. It bunched up underneath her white knuckles and blood drained from her face leaving her almost as pale as Drakkus.

"Kor?"

Not a question.

Just my name.

That was all Rayka said as I stood there. And yet, I knew she sought an answer. An answer I couldn't very well give her because I didn't know it myself. I didn't know what had compelled me to return or how I'd even known to find the place again in the labyrinth that made up the streets of Abirell. The blood bond, perhaps. But I knew that wasn't fully it. There was some other force, something greater than my understanding, that had dragged my feet back to the place.

"Will he die?" I asked, my voice callous and cold.

Rayka opened her mouth to answer me, but her eyes drifted past me and widened. Beside me, Otho scrambled to his feet, letting the stick he was carving fall to the ground with a thump.

I turned at the sound of footsteps behind me and found myself staring up at Jarris' face. It was blank, no expression revealing his thoughts as he stopped and looked over my shoulder at Drakkus. I'd seen that careful vacancy in his expression before. Typically, right before Jarris made a kill. My eyes trailed down to his hand and I saw it resting with seeming nonchalance on the hilt of his largest knife.

"Should he?" Jarris asked, breaking the tense silence that surrounded his appearance.

That question hung in the air.

"I... I," I stammered, caught off guard and perplexed by the question. Perplexed by the reaction inside of me at it. Did I want Drakkus to die? Wasn't that why I hadn't warned him of the attack I knew was coming? A word from me to Jarris and it would be done. I knew that. But I couldn't say it.

"No," Rayka said. "No."

"They're the ones who took you?"

A growing uneasiness kept me silent, but I nodded at Jarris' inquiry.

Jarris moved with lightning speed, crossing the short distance between him and Otho. He gave Otho no time to react, no time to move out of his reach, before snatching up Otho's arm and holding it up. It was the scar on his hand that Jarris was looking at.

My brother motioned me toward him with his free hand. I stepped up to him and let him grab my wrist. He studied the scars that marked both Otho and I's palms, his lips pursed in a troubled frown.

They were identical.

"This was where you were yesterday?"

I nodded again, jerking my hand away from him.

"And this was why you were asking about blood bonds?"

"I guess so."

Jarris released his hold on Otho, who backed away as quickly as he could, and turned his attention to Drakkus. Rayka rose from her chair, her face white.

"He's the one who did that to you?"

"Yes," I said.

"Then that is the answer to my question, isn't it?" So simply. As if a few questions of his own could answer the question I'd wrestled with for months.

"No," Rayka said again. "We have wronged Korris, that is true. But it was never meant badly. We never meant for any harm to come to him."

"No harm? You stole my brother. You dragged him north with you into the mountains. You performed a blood ritual on him. A blood ritual that is forbidden among our people. He," Jarris gestured toward Drakkus' inert body, "did that to Korris. Which means I've every right to take his life."

His knife was in his hand before he was finished speaking. That terrible blank calm was back on his face, an emptiness that belied the deadly anger underneath. My brother had never been very forgiving. Less than two steps separated him from Drakkus and Rayka was no obstacle to Jarris. Less than two steps and blood would flow.

My stomach twisted as I stared at the cold gleam of the blade in my brother's hand, the memory of another knife sliding through my hand awakened by the sight of it. Followed by more memories. Of Borssa's excitement. Of Otho's graying face. Of pain and fear that churned beneath the numbness. Of Drakkus' growing alarm as the long hours of that night wore on. Of Destiny and her strange words.

The uneasiness inside me drowned out even my anger. I couldn't watch Drakkus die. The thought made me ill.

"Jarris, stop."

Rayka, Otho and Jarris all turned and stared at me.

"Korris...," Jarris started, the first sign of doubt breaking through his icy exterior.

I shut my eyes. "No. Stop."

"They hurt you. They tried to steal from you."

Neither Rayka nor Otho spoke up in their own defense. Their silence lent the air a certain tension that worsened the sick feeling inside of me. They made no denial against the claims Jarris made. They made no excuses. I think if they had, if they had tried to argue against the truth of what they'd done to me, I might have surrendered to Jarris' revenge.

"I don't care, Jarris. I just can't watch it. I can't watch you kill him." He opened his mouth, but I didn't give him a chance to speak. Now that I was giving voice to the weight I never lived without, I couldn't stop. "Just don't kill him. I'm tired of watching people die. It's all I ever see. Every vision, everywhere I go, people die. I'm sick of it. I just want it to end." I never meant to say so much but the words came out without waiting for my permission. So much death. The world's end. Abirell's destruction. Drakkus' camp. Dragon's Nest. I was beginning to feel like Brym, with death clinging to my bones despite the life inside me. A shadow I could not rid myself of. It wasn't that I was desperate for Drakkus to live. Just that I did not want to see him die. As the words fled out of me, a weariness took hold of me. "Please, Jarris. I hate them all more than you ever can, but I can't watch anymore death."

I had a hold of my brother's arm, gripping it with both my hands to stop him from bringing his knife up, hoping that he would understand my desperate desire. Hoping that he would understand that it wasn't acceptance of what they'd done to me, just a need to not witness another death.

Outside the open door, the birds had gone quiet. Outside the open door, a stillness hung in the air, every bit as taut as the stillness inside that room as Jarris stared down at me trying to decide how seriously to take my outburst.

Outside the open door, a distant wail broke through that stillness.

I tugged at his arm, pulling him back a step.

"Let's just go. Let's just get out of here. I shouldn't have come here in the first place."

Something was happening outside. The stillness was broken by faint shouts, the tramp of running feet.

Inside, Rayka and Otho were still just staring at me, dumbfounded by my sudden defense of Drakkus. Jarris still had his knife in his hand, but he was backing away at my urging, toward the door, confusion spilling over onto his face. I knew he heard what I heard outside, and he was trying to piece it together.

Some of the shouts were getting closer. The words on the very edge of my hearing. There was a desperation in those shouts. A fear. A horror. The sound of them turned me cold.

"We need to go, Jarris," I said, my voice coming out a whisper. "We need to get out of here. Now."

For I heard one word rise out above all the others - plague.

Plague in the city.

As the meaning of that single word sank into me, I dropped Jarris' arm and backed all the way to the door, shaking my head in silent, useless denial. It couldn't be. I'd seen them kill the Outlander. Jarris had seen them kill the Outlander. And there had only ever been that one. Hadn't there?

Inside my head, I heard Brym's soft laughter. It echoed through the recesses of my mind, crazed and wild.

I stumbled a little as I backed up, my head between my hands, desperate to run from the sound of her laughter but it followed me. You can't outrun something that's inside of you.

"We have to go, Jarris," I said again, louder. "We have to go. It's happening."

"What's happening?"

"Plague. There's plague here," Otho answered for me, his eyes meeting mine with understanding. "Just like your vision."

"But that shouldn't be possible. Orle killed that creature."

"Does it matter how it's possible?" I said. "It's here. The plague's here. And... and... Jarris, it kills everyone."

Outside, the noise was swelling. When I said the words a second time, I felt them. I felt the weight of them, the guilt. There was plague in Abirell after all. The same plague I'd told Brym to use to spare myself the beating Harysh would give me and to spare myself from having to witness one of Drakkus' men eaten by an Outlander. There was plague in the city, and it was my fault and I'd been a fool to think killing Brym, killing her monster, would be enough to halt the plans she'd been several lifetimes making.

I remembered the sound of her voice, full of glee, coming from the creature that had hunted Jarris and I, driving us closer and closer until Abirell seemed like the safest choice and I realized that she had always planned it so. I hadn't just told her how to make Abirell fall. Somehow, I'd led her monster to it.

Her laughter in my head grew louder. The same laughter I'd heard come from her in the moments before she died.

"She's dead," I murmured to myself, trying to convince my own mind of the truth. "She's dead."

I clamped my hands over my ears, trying to block out not only the sound of her mad laughter but the sounds that were coming from outside in the city as well. There was panic in the air. If the plague traveled half as fast as the fear of it did, then there was little hope for anyone inside the walls of Abirell.

Including us.

Jarris stood, doubt and indecision stamped on his face. He looked between Otho and I and hesitated. I wanted to yell at him to hurry, to stop wasting precious time. Before I could, he came to a decision and moved.

His knife was no longer lowered but raised, pressed tight against Otho's throat. Jarris stood behind Otho, one arm pinning Otho against him. I stared, not at my brother or Otho, but at the knife as it formed an indent on Otho's neck. I heard Otho draw in a sharp, strangled breath and saw his eyes widen in fear.

"You're coming with us," Jarris said.

Otho tried to pull away but my brother's grip around him was unyielding. All his efforts accomplished was driving the blade of the knife deeper into his skin, drawing a thin trickle of blood. His face twisted a little as he felt the sting of that cut.

"I'm not going anywhere with you," Otho managed to get out.

"You're blood bound to each other. If you die, so might he and that's not a chance I'm taking."

"You can't just make me go with you," Otho protested, his gaze torn between Jarris and Rayka.

"Jarris, let's just go," I said.

Jarris responded by tightening his hold on Otho and, with the encouragement of his knife, backed toward the door, dragging a very unwilling Otho with him.

"I'm not going with you," Otho said, his face pale but set. He tried to break free of Jarris' hold once more.

It was Rayka who ended what might have been a stalemate. She had said nothing for several minutes and to my surprise it wasn't Otho and Jarris she was watching, but me.

"Go with them, Otho," she said quietly.

"What? No. I'm not leaving you and Father. You need..."

"He's right." Rayka glanced at Jarris and then back at me. "You can't die."

Although I doubted that Rayka wished any harm to come to me, I was quite certain that her greatest interest in that moment was getting Otho safely out of the city. And if that meant sending him with us, she would do just that. By the dark look on Otho's face, I'm sure he guessed the same. He made no effort to cooperate with Jarris, though.

"What about you?"

"We'll follow. As we are able. But to risk your life is to risk his and that is our fault."

I edged nearer the door, the tumult from the other parts of the city spilling into the streets around us. I could hear the word plague passed from person to person, as contagious as the disease itself was.

Since I'd only seen it at work once, I wasn't sure just how fast its spread would be in the city. My vision had only shown me the aftermath, the eerie stillness on the streets filled with dead bodies. How long it took to reach that, I could not say.

"We don't have time for this," I said, standing in the doorway watching as people, many carrying as many of their possessions as they could manage, filled the street. If the people of Abirell felt it necessary to leave their homes behind at once, I didn't think it wise to delay our own departure. "We need to go."

"Go, Otho," Rayka said again. Her voice was quiet still but firm and steady. There was no argument that would change her mind. "We will find you."

Chapter 14

I WAS RUNNING DOWN THE hallway of the governor's house with Rensi's accusation pounding through my head, stoked to life once more.

"You are Fentra's curse."

Rensi's voice, filled with a mixture of awe and fear, came to mind. They weren't the sort of words I wished to think about just then, but, coupled with Brym's mad laughter that rose to the surface of my mind, they were impossible to set aside and ignore.

Throughout the entire house, there was a hush that belied the furor that held the rest of Abirell captive. In the yard down below, Jarris and Otho were preparing the horses. I had seen nothing of either Semptius or Captain Orle in my mad dash through the house to our room.

Inside our room, I slammed the door shut and leaned my back against it, temporarily forgetting my need for haste. An ache was forming in the center of my head, and I rubbed at my forehead with one palm. The vision might still have been hours away, but I cursed its presence just then. The Fates cared so little for choosing convenient times to interrupt my life. It made me wonder sometimes if that was how I would meet my end someday - too lost in the throes of the future to survive some event of the present.

There was a bit of irony in that thought.

Jarris was waiting for me, I reminded myself, and set about the rather simple task of collecting the few items we'd brought with us, mostly Jarris' extra weapons and clothes that he'd had with him. There was nothing of mine to collect. Balia had burned my old, worn clothes without bothering to ask me and my only other possessions were the two knives Rensi had given me and Brym's periapt. I wore all three constantly.

"Korris," Semptius said, stepping into the room behind me. I spun around, startled. I hadn't heard him enter. "You are leaving? Good. It is for the best. Although I shall always be sorry to have your stay so cruelly interrupted."

I stood, shame for my own part in Abirell's demise rolling over me, unable to meet the man's eyes. "Will you be able to stop it?"

"Yes. But it is best if you don't ask how, Korris."

Since that was exactly what my next question would have been, I remained silent.

"Don't look so despondent. The day may come when you get to return here in peace and without threat of plague or any other violence," Semptius said, conjuring up a sad smile that did little to comfort me. "Here. Take this. I know you cannot read it yourself but perhaps you will find yourself in company with someone who can read it to you."

I looked down at what he offered. It was a book, much thinner than some of those I'd seen him reading. Faded marks were etched across the worn leather cover and the edges of the pages were yellowed as if someone had spent a great deal of time thumbing through it.

"What is it?"

"It's about the last days of Fentra. You were so interested in her, I thought you might like it. And there are things in there, perhaps, that you should know. Things you should learn about your predecessor." He pushed it into my hands. "You should hurry. Plague is like wildfire once it begins."

I swallowed down my own guilt, although the pain of it only tightened its hold on me. I didn't deserve his kindness just then. Not when I was the reason for the plague. The fact that he was giving one of his precious books up spoke of how little hope he had.

"Are you leaving too?" I asked, still staring down at the book in my hands to avoid his eyes.

"No. I think we might still be able to save the city but even if we cannot, my place is here with my people." His sad smile flitted across his face again and it hurt to see it.

His words filled me with a sorrow I'd never felt before. And that made me anxious to get away from him, to put distance between myself and what I knew would likely happen. Abirell wasn't saved in my vision. And if he insisted on remaining behind, he wouldn't be, either.

"Jarris is waiting," I blurted out, heading for the door with the small bundle of belongings I'd collected and the book Semptius had given me.

"Yes. Go to him. And may the Fates guide you safely." He paused. "And if we are fortunate to ever meet again, Korris, I hope it will be under far better circumstances."

~   ~   ~

The tumult in the streets was getting louder, getting closer. Panic was in the air and was closing in fast. I tucked the thin book into one of the numerous packs the horse carried, rubbed a final time at the ache in my head and stepped into the stirrup of my own mount while Jarris held its head.

The streets that had been so hushed and deserted when we first came into Abirell two evenings before were now in chaos. The inner parts of the city, around the governor's house, were yet untouched by the plague. People flocked to the streets, many with only what they could carry. I'd only ever seen that many people gathered together like that one other time - our arrival at Dragon's Nest. Rather than move toward the gates, though, this crowd withdrew deeper into the city, nearer to the sea. The crowd was so thick, I doubted we'd get our horses through it, but Jarris didn't lead us after the crowd. He turned his horse's head toward the gate. Toward the nearly deserted front of the city.

There were soldiers spread out in the road in front of us, rolling out great wooden barrels and pouring the contents of those barrels out onto the street. Black powdery dust.

Jarris spurred his horse into a gallop and Otho and I followed. We tore past the soldiers spreading firedust and past the handful of people who wandered aimlessly around beyond them. I barely gave those people thought until we neared the gate, and I noticed one of them whose skin was almost completely white with plague. They turned and watched us as we raced past them, their eyes as white as their skin and glazed over.

"Jarris?"

"Don't stop," Jarris called over his shoulder as he neared the opening gate.

There were more soldiers outside the gate, and they had evidently been made aware of our approach. The gates opened only enough for us to pass through and then were sealed shut behind us. Jarris didn't slow his horse. We galloped straight up the small rise in front of Abirell and I turned back.

It was a mistake.

Blue and orange flames leaped to life in the part of the city near the gate and even at that distance, I heard the wail that rose from within the flames. I yanked my reins hard, bringing my horse to a stop as I sat and watched the fire.

"They're doing what they have to, Korris," Jarris said quietly, drawing his own horse to a stop beside mine. I could feel his eyes on me but I couldn't tear my own eyes off the distant fire. "If they can burn it out, they can stop its spread. And as long as they contain the fire, they can spare the rest of the city."

Sacrificing the few to save the many.

A choice I had been too cowardly to make.

A choice I'd forced them to make.

"This is all my fault," I said, my voice hoarse and catching. I caught Otho's eyes as the words left my mouth and there was a question in them that I didn't want him knowing the answer to.

I'd never hated my gift more than I did in that moment, watching as flames consumed the infected part of Abirell and the people who were inside it.

It wasn't like Dragon's Nest where I could find no pity for those who had chanted for our deaths. There had been a ruthless sort of satisfaction in watching Dragon's Nest burn.

It wasn't even like watching Drakkus and his men cut down after what they'd done to me. There had been a callous sort of justice in that moment.

But Abirell had welcomed us. Sheltered us. Had offered a freedom that I'd never experienced before, not even among my own people. They were something different and now they burned.

And Semptius, who ruled without a periapt, who loved his books. Semptius had welcomed me, without trying to use me. He was unlike any leader I'd ever met.

It made me ache in a horrible, hollow way to think of what I'd brought on them.

I stared and stared at the distant flames; their crackle fierce enough to reach our ears even as far away as we were. On one side of me, Otho watched the burning city just as intently as I did. On the other side of me, Jarris watched me.

"Come on, Korris," Jarris said at last, reaching for my horse's bridle. "We have a long way to go."

He didn't understand my words because I'd never told him what I'd given to Brym. That weight was mine and mine alone. At least, until I remembered that Otho had seen every future I had. He might not know that I'd given Brym the idea, but he most certainly knew that I'd seen this future. The burden of that guilt would go with me to my grave.

A final glance at Abirell, wreathed in raging flame with black plumes of smoke darkening the sky above her and blocking our view of the city beyond the burning part, and that image was forever engraved in my mind.

~   ~   ~

Jarris was quiet.

Too quiet.

In the hours we'd spent riding hard, putting as much distance between us and Abirell, there hadn't been a good chance for any of us to speak.

That excuse disappeared as soon as we made camp for the night under the canopy of a single, spindly tree, whose branches grew almost all to one side thanks to the constant wind that swept the plains. Small, bright leaves were slowly unfurling themselves on the branches and a bird's nest was nestled into the fork of two branches. Pink and white blossoms sweetened the air around us and promised a harvest of fruit to whoever happened to pass by the tree in a few months.

There was a stream nearby, swollen with spring rains, rushing madly on its way to the nearest river. If I could have erased the morning's events from my mind, the scene would have been as tranquil as any I'd known. Nature around us held no hint of the destruction that had taken place only a few hours away.

Still, Jarris said nothing. His face was also carefully devoid of any expression. Whatever was going on inside his mind, he was intent on keeping to himself.

Jarris lit a fire while Otho and I took care of the horses, a task that was difficult due to the growing pain in my head. The vision would come that night, I was sure. I shot a glance in Otho's direction, curious if he felt the same onset of pain as I did or if the arrival of my visions caught him completely by surprise each time. He avoided my eyes, robbing me of any chance to make a good guess.

Finished with the horses, I sat down near the fire and cradled my head with one hand, wondering what death and destruction the Fates would choose to show me this time. It was always death and destruction. After Abirell, I wasn't sure if I could bear anymore. I didn't want to bear anymore.

Staring into the flames made something twist up inside of me and I scooted back away from the fire, suddenly appalled at its destructive nature. Appalled at how voracious it was and how easily it could kill.

"What happened in Abirell wasn't your fault, Korris," Jarris said, breaking his long silence. He had a skewer of meat held over the fire and the smell of roasting flesh nauseated me.

Turning away from the smell of it and the sight of the fire, I said nothing. I wished Otho wasn't there, seated awkwardly at some distance from either of us and clearly unsure of what to do. The little bit of blood Jarris had drawn from his neck had dried in a smeared streak, its color stark against the paleness of his skin. He hadn't said a word, either, since leaving Abirell behind.

We sat there, the three of us, each silent and too absorbed in our own thoughts, our own troubles to speak to each other. The fire crackled and hissed and popped, and I moved further away from it. The meat hanging over the flame sizzled and smoked and filled the air with a smell I could not tolerate although it was one that I'd grown up with.

"Here, eat," Jarris said, when the meat was cooked.

I shook my head, pressing my lips together to keep from gagging.

"You haven't eaten since this morning."

"Not hungry."

Jarris shrugged instead of arguing with me and tore a piece of meat off for himself.

"You might as well come eat," he called out to Otho.

Otho glared at him, his jaw set in grim determination, and made no move.

"What? Are you both planning on starving yourselves?" Jarris asked, looking between the two of us. His gaze settled on Otho who tried and failed to maintain the ferocity of his glare. "I just saved your life dragging you out of there. You know that, don't you?"

"I didn't ask you to."

"Just get over here and eat."

Otho got up and shuffled to a spot nearer the fire. He kept his eyes down, avoiding both Jarris and I, but even so, I could see that it was more than just our presence that was bothering him. From time to time as he sat there eating, he turned, craning his neck to look over his shoulder as if he expected Drakkus and Rayka to show up on the distant horizon. Each time the horizon remained empty, and he slumped further and further into a despair I well understood.

Even without the blood bond that prevented my anger toward him, I would have been hard pressed to stay angry with him under the circumstances. He was easier to pity than Rensi had been - probably due to Rensi's insistence on keeping me tethered to her.

I sat back against the tree, nursing the growing pain in my head and watching Jarris and Otho as they partook of their silent meal. Otho, when he wasn't looking over his shoulder, stole frequent glances at me. I wondered again if he felt the same pain I did when a vision got near. Before I could ask, though, the vision came.

Chapter 15

I T WAS STRANGE, THAT VISION.

Quiet.

Not the silence that accompanied my time walking when I was restricted to just my sense of sight. Instead, it was the quiet of a peaceful summer night. The soft hooting of owls, the chirping of a thousand crickets. The gentle rustle of wind moving through leaves. The rhythmic pulse of little waves breaking on the shore.

There was none of the screaming that came with my fiery one, none of the eerie silence that haunted the one about Abirell.

It was just... peaceful.

All I saw at first was a dark room. All I felt was a night chill in the air. There was a large bed in that room, its wooden frame and posts carved in beautiful designs. A large wardrobe in the corner. Moonlight broke free from the cloud it was hiding behind and flooded the room with silvery light, revealing a beautifully woven carpet full of rich colors. The moonlight glinted softly off of golden candlesticks.

A man and woman were sleeping in the bed, their still forms visible in the pale new light. A peaceful scene, without any sense of foreboding at first. I wondered what significance it had that the Fates had sent it.

And then there were footsteps, light as a hunter's. They came creeping across that room and a third person was entering the vision. A person clad in long, flowing robes that were as dark as the night around them. They were moving with stealth, their presence a secret to the sleeping couple. In their hand was a knife. The blade, sharp and cold looking. From somewhere beyond my sight, an infant was crying.

The assassin was at the bed, hovering over the woman's body. Clamping one hand over her mouth as the other drew the knife in a single slashing motion across her throat. There was a soft gurgle of blood, not enough to wake the man beside her.

The killer was moving to the other side with as much care as before but just as they reached it, the man woke. The assassin was trying to pin him down and the man was reaching for something on the small bedside table - something red and glowing faintly. The struggle, lasting only moments, ended with the knife through the man's heart.

Their work completed, the assassin was turning to leave, and I caught a brief glimpse of the face beneath the hood of their robe. It was a man's face, a thin, white scar running down the center of it, clipping off part of his nose and pulling one side of his lip up in a permanent sneer. It was the sort of face not easily forgotten.

That was the final image of my vision. It wavered, watery, before my eyes and then melted away, depositing me back into the present.

Night had fallen fully, although the fire burned brightly enough that I could see my immediate surroundings. I was lying on my side, my face pressed against the dirt. Jarris and Otho both sat on the other side of the fire, the flickering light of the fire playing with the shadows on their faces.

Otho was leaning forward, his elbows resting on his knees and his hands holding his head up on either side. It took me a moment of staring at him to realize that his eyes were squeezed shut as if in pain.

"Back again?" Jarris asked.

I pushed myself up off the ground and nodded, wincing at the pain it caused me, not quite ready to speak. Not ready to share what I'd seen. Not sure what I made of it. I was used to the pain that lingered after a vision. I was used to the disorienting moments that followed one. But nothing had prepared me for the hollowness that came on the heels of my latest sight.

S. T. Hobbs

Glad that I had chosen to sit against the tree, I leaned my aching head back on the rough bark and shut my eyes. I knew Jarris wouldn't ask about my vision. He never did. Instead, he poked at the fire, stirring it up and sending sparks floating up into the night sky above us.

"You should eat, Korris," he said after we'd sat in silence for several minutes.

"Still not hungry," I muttered.

It was true, too. My appetite was lost the second I let my thoughts turn to Abirell. Even the strangeness of the vision couldn't erase the weight of that. With my eyes shut, I could picture my final sight of the city, its wood succumbing quickly to the ravages of the fire. To my eyes, it seemed impossible to control such a flame. I could well imagine it devouring the entire city and still being hungry for more.

For a moment, I was tempted to find Semptius' thread of time. I was tempted to follow it and see if it had survived the purge of flame. The temptation lasted only a moment, lost almost at once to the prospect of witnessing his death. I couldn't do that. Not after all the other deaths I'd been a spectator to. Not after all the kindness he'd shown me.

"I should have stayed in Abirell," Otho said quietly, as if talking to himself and not really meaning for Jarris and me to hear.

Even in the darkness, I could see the paleness of Otho's face. His eyes widened briefly as he met mine and then dropped and I shifted uncomfortably with the reminder that he'd just seen the same vision I had.

"What you should have done was not take Korris, then we might have made it a few more years before this mess started."

I frowned and laid back down, my head aching too badly to question Jarris' words, although I desperately wanted to, and I promised myself that I would just as soon as I was feeling better.

"You can't blame me for what's happening now."

"None of it was happening before you and your family took him."

For the sake of my head, I wished they would be quiet. The pain was too intense to even hope for sleep, but silence would have been nice.

"We didn't start this," Otho insisted, his face flushed hot. "It was all going to happen anyway."

"In a few years."

Otho let out a groan of frustration. "I didn't hurt your brother. And that night was far worse for me than it was him."

I wanted to protest that claim, but my head ached too badly. He might have had to suffer all my visions in one night, but at least no one was attempting to rip something out of him and give it to another. Even as that thought came to me, it evaporated, turning it into pity that he'd lived through so much in one night. And that angered me, even if I could not let that anger out on Otho. It festered inside me as they continued to argue.

"Does it matter? You tried to steal his gift."

"Because it should have been mine. We weren't trying to hurt him. Father said it was the only way."

"Stealing his gift was the only way? Do you have any idea what that's like?"

Otho gave a helpless shrug. "It was just his gift. He would have been fine still without. Better even. He wouldn't have ever had to worry about being used for it again."

Jarris' mouth hung open for just a moment. A heated flush filled his face and I worried that he might forget all about Otho and I's blood bond and kill Otho right then and there. Surely, the thought came to him. I saw his hand resting, waiting on the hilt of his knife.

When he spoke again, his voice was soft and lethal. "If I cut your arm off because I think it should be mine instead of yours, would it be better?"

"It's not the same. It's not like that."

"It's exactly like that. You take something away that someone was born with, that they've had their whole lives, and you leave them a cripple, forever missing a piece of themselves. That's what you and your father tried to do to Korris and there is no reason in the world that makes that right. None. You would have left him a mutilated, wrecked version of himself."

Otho's head dropped as Jarris spoke. His fingers found handfuls of grass to rip up and tear into little pieces as he suffered under Jarris' wrath. He at least had the decency to glance, ashamed, at me. I met his stare with indifference, which was the best I could do at the moment.

"You would have, too, if your father had told you to. The world's ending and there isn't any other way to stop it."

His words gave Jarris pause to think. Lying on my side, I watched as doubt flitted across my brother's face. It cleared a moment later and he shook his head.

"No. I don't care who told me to do it, I wouldn't have gone along with it. You don't get to decide the sacrifices other people make to solve anything."

I could see Otho wanted to speak again and wanted to defend both himself and his family. But Jarris' words had torn to pieces any argument or excuse he could make. His fingers closed tightly about the handful of shredded grass he hadn't tossed back onto the ground yet and he glanced at me again.

I wasn't sure what he wanted from me. I might not have been able to be angry with him, but I certainly didn't plan on defending him against my brother, either. Perhaps it was a little cruel of Jarris to lay out the truth of what they'd tried to do in such a scathing manner only hours after Otho had been forced away from his own family. I tried to shove that thought away as soon as it entered, sure that it came only from our blood bond.

"Why would giving you Korris' foresight change anything?" Jarris asked when it became clear that Otho had no intention of speaking out again.

"Because in three hundred years, I'm the only firstborn of a king to have survived more than my first winter." Confusion entered Otho's face for the first time. Turning his head away from us and staring at the western horizon, he sighed. "Kor's gift should have wanted to come to me. It should have worked."

I think Jarris truly had no idea what to say to that. I certainly didn't. And yet, when the silence was broken again, it was by me. "You're really the only one who survived more than a year?"

Otho was staring at the ground, still tearing handfuls of grass out and ripping it to shreds. He nodded.

"How?"

"Because they lied about me." Otho's voice softened as he said, "You shouldn't have made me leave them."

"And if we'd left you behind and you'd died, Korris might have died as well. Like I said, that's not a risk I'm willing to take. Besides, it's only fair. A son for a son."

"Just let him be, Jarris," I mumbled, annoyed by the loudness of their argument. "None of this was his fault."

Jarris gave me a funny look, tilting his head a bit to one side as he studied me. "Why are you on his side? He tried to take your gift."

Neither Otho nor I said anything for a moment, only looked at each other. Jarris was right. I ought to have been upset with Otho. I ought to have taken up Jarris' side, not Otho's. It irritated me that I hadn't, but even that irritation could not be directed toward Otho. It was that exchange of glances that sealed Jarris' suspicion. He crossed his arms over his chest.

"It's the blood bond, isn't it?"

I nodded from where I lay while Otho winced and said, "I think so."

"Exactly how much do you share?"

I hadn't found anything of Otho's that I shared, so once more I remained quiet.

"I," Otho looked down at his hands that were busy tearing a blade of new green grass into tiny pieces, "I share his visions."

"What do you mean? You have the gift of foresight too?"

"No. Not like Kor does. I just see whatever he sees, whenever he sees it. Nothing on my own, though. I don't think we share anything else. At least, if we do, I haven't found it yet."

"And apparently, you can't be enemies, either."

To that both Otho and I simply nodded. Remembering how hard I'd tried to hate him after first learning about the bond, I felt at least a slight satisfaction in knowing that Otho couldn't despise me either.

I wasn't sure if he would have without the bond. He hadn't seemed to that night on the mountaintop but perhaps that was just the work of the blood bond already beginning.

Jarris just put his head in his hands. The loud sigh that escaped him held a hint of a groan in it.

"Isn't that wonderful?" he said a moment later. "Now I just have to make sure to keep both of you alive. I think our trip to the Iron Towers just got even longer."

"I can take care of myself," Otho said, bristling with indignance at Jarris' tone of aggravation.

Jarris lifted his head out of his hands long enough to fix him with a dour glare. "By choosing to stay somewhere you would most likely die? A brilliant choice. Yes, I can see how well you can take care of yourself."

"You don't know that we're that bonded."

"You don't know that you're not. And how do you think we should find out?" Jarris gave the fire one last jab with his stick before tossing it into the flames. "Let you die and hope Korris doesn't go with you? It'd be a little late to change anything, then, wouldn't it?"

Otho had nothing to say to that.

Nor did I.

Jarris glanced from one of us to the other, shaking his head and muttering something under his breath.

I couldn't help but feel a little sorry for my eldest brother. It really was a long way back to the Iron Towers. And Jarris felt duty bound to ensure my safety every step of the way, which meant he had to ensure Otho's as well. I tried to think of something, anything, to say that would make all of it better, but there wasn't anything.

~ ~ ~

The night was half spent by the time I convinced Jarris that I was not sleeping and that he might as well. He'd felt nothing approach our camp in the hours since we'd stopped and that was the best we could hope for. Otho was already asleep, or feigning sleep to keep us from bringing him into any more conversations.

Once persuaded, Jarris was quick to fall asleep and I was left to myself. Left to sort through my recent vision and through our brief time at Abirell.

Going to the horses, I pulled out the thin book Semptius had given me. I couldn't hope to read it. The markings on it were just that - markings. They meant nothing to me. But the gift did. The kindness meant a great deal to me, especially since I could never hope to repay it.

It fell open on my lap to a page that was more than just senseless markings. There was a drawing of a woman's face. The ink was smudged and faded after so many years, but I guessed that the picture was meant to be Fentra. The flickering of the firelight made the picture move with the shadows, fascinating me. Her eyes, one of the clearest parts of the picture, were sad. There was no smile on her face.

I wondered how long before her death the picture had been drawn, if perhaps she already knew that most people wanted her dead. Or if her sadness came from something else – perhaps a vision not unlike my one about Abirell's fall.

I skimmed my fingertips over the markings on the next page, awed by the fact that there were people who could look at them and make sense of them. Perhaps that was as much of a gift as tracking or foresight. If it was, I would have preferred it to my own.

"Who was that in your vision?" Otho asked, his voice barely a whisper but still startling me.

"I have no idea." I glanced over in his direction and found him sitting up, not the slightest trace of sleep on his face.

"Don't you wonder who they were?"

I shrugged. "Does it matter?"

"If you could warn them..."

"I can't. Besides, I don't think warning does any good."

Otho moved closer, sitting beside me, and looking over my shoulder at the book spread across my lap. My first thought was to slam it shut, to keep it to myself even if I had no idea what its pages said. I admitted to myself that it was a ridiculous thought and left the book open.

"I thought you were asleep," I said.

"As if I could be." His eyes darted over to where Jarris lay. "Your brother is terrifying. Not sure I'll ever be able to sleep around him."

"Yes, he is," I agreed, glancing at Jarris' sleeping form.

"You knew about the attack on Father's camp."

Otho's words took me by surprise. It was no question. And there was no malice or bitterness in his voice. Just an acknowledgement of the fact. I nodded, staring down at the book because I didn't want to meet his eyes. To be honest, I'd forgotten that he would have seen the vision that foretold the attack.

"You didn't try to warn him."

Again, it was no question and so I made no answer. It did no good to try to deny the fact. I sucked in a breath and held it, waiting for his accusation, waiting for the sharp words that would remind me of Rensi's when she found out.

"I guess I probably wouldn't have, either."

I turned my head to look at him sitting beside me, trying to read his expression through the darkness. It held not even a hint of the anger Rensi had expressed. Even with our blood bond, I'd expected something closer to Rensi's reaction from him. He'd been rather hateful to me before the ritual. I wondered what had changed. There was more different about him than just the blood bond.

"Jarris was right," I said at last. "You shouldn't have taken me. Then maybe you could still be with your family. And I'd be with mine."

The sigh Otho let out was barely audible, but I knew my words had cut, even without the sharpness of anger behind them. In a single, fleeting moment, the thought came to me to walk Rayka or Drakkus' time and let Otho see what had happened to his parents. But I didn't do it. Because, blood bond or no, I wasn't walking time for anyone ever again.

"If neither of you are going to sleep, we might as well keep going," Jarris said, sitting up. He looked between the two of us and shook his head again, a look in his eyes that told us he'd heard the entire conversation. "It's a long way to the Iron Towers."

"You can't take Kor there."

Jarris gave Otho a questioning look.

"Queen Cholla will..."

"Oh, yes. I know all about Queen Cholla and how much she hates the gifted, but she's always had agreements with the tribes about them. Korris is safe as long as he stays with our tribe." Jarris looked from Otho to me. "And don't you both start arguing with me."

CHAPTER 16

~Rensi's Writings~

*I*T'S THE MIDDLE OF THE NIGHT as I write this but sleep's my enemy right now. I hate the dreams that come with it sometimes. Tonight, I dreamed of that final night in Dragon's Nest. What I did that night I can never tell anyone, and so I shall write it here.

I killed someone that night.

I killed Harysh and I don't feel one bit bad about it.

Sometimes it frightens me how indifferent I am to the fact that I killed a man. He deserved it, though. Sometimes I think that indifference is what Kor must have felt when he knew Father would die and said nothing. Although Father never did to Kor anything like what Harysh did to me.

He was standing over me that night as he had so many other times. I guess he thought I'd never fight

143

back. I guess he forgot that every time he touched me he just made me hate him more. He forgot a lot of things, actually. He was a fool, really. I wonder why Brym even bothered to keep him around. Mostly, he just forgot that Father's periapt that I kept was more than just a periapt. He forgot it was a knife. Or maybe he didn't forget. Maybe he really just thought I couldn't do it.

He was wrong, of course.

But that doesn't make the nightmares any easier. In my nightmares, I fail. Or I succeed. When I fail, I wake up wondering if it would have been for the best. If less people would have died. If I had truly failed, Kor and I would still be in Dragon's Nest, there would still be a Dragon's Nest, and the Outlanders would not be freely roaming the plains.

I almost hate the times, like tonight, when I succeed again in my dreams. There's always so much blood. More than there really was. And Harysh makes the most awful sounds but that's not what bothers me. What bothers me every time is the look I see on Kor's face when I first find him afterwards. That's part of the dream, usually, but it's also part of reality. He stared at me as if I was one of those creatures Brym kept in the dark in her cavern. Of course, after what he began in Dragon's Nest, I think I stared at him the same way.

I do wish, more with every passing day, that Mother and Otho would arrive. Jahniss and Naleiah try hard to make up for their absence, but all the things we used to do together are no longer of much interest to me. I missed all the parties and the dancing and the feasting when we were out in the plains, but now that I've come back, it seems as if they lost all their appeal. Likely because I can't ignore the things I know are happening outside of Ludys. I know that we're not as safe as everyone pretends we are. Only Uncle Mitkas seems to share that knowledge. He almost never smiles and he spends more and more time each day alone, muttering to himself and pouring over letters and books.

Jahniss is hosting another banquet tomorrow in honor of the Planting Moon. She shall expect me to attend, I'm sure, and so I really should try to sleep now. The Fates know, her banquets last well nigh the whole night.

CHAPTER 17

I 'D FORGOTTEN TO GIVE THE vial of dragon's blood back to Semptius.

I was a thief, but I hadn't meant to be. It made me wonder if being a thief was just another part of Fentra's curse that Rensi thought I was.

I balanced the periapt on one finger, watching it tilt gently from side to side, the liquid sliding smoothly along the cylindrical interior. The longer I toyed with the useless periapt, the more I noticed about it. It emitted a faint hum that was almost inaudible unless I held it right up to my ear.

I pulled Brym's periapt out and held that up to my ear to compare the two, but it made no sound. Just like it gave off no colored glow. Compared to the dragon's blood, even the flecks of gold inside the eye of a dragon were less dazzling than they had been when I'd first seen them.

Replacing both periapts, one inside my shirt and the other in a pocket, I rose and started helping Jarris ready our horses for the day's ride.

We'd been riding away from Abirell, or what remained of Abirell, for two days. In those two days, Otho hadn't stopped watching the western horizon. In two days, we hadn't seen a single other person follow us on our retreat from Abirell. Most of the people had been hurrying deeper into the city, nearer to the sea.

After two days, it was beginning to feel as if we were the only three left in the world. The plains were empty all around us, devoid even of the flocks of migrating birds and herds of horses and deer that usually ventured out into the open grasslands just as soon as winter had ended.

Jarris gave me a quick, sharp look when I reached him and the horses. I ignored it and began buckling the saddle onto my own mount.

"You know, the plague would have reached them whether we went there or not," he said carefully, broaching a topic I'd been reluctant to speak on in those last two days.

Actually, I'd been quite reticent about a lot of things, preferring to not speak at all. There were too many cracks inside me, too many bits and pieces that I couldn't sort out. Abirell was my fault. Which meant Rensi might have been right in accusing me of being Fentra's curse. Which meant that I wasn't sure what to do or what course to follow since death seemed to accompany me everywhere I went.

Then there was my most recent vision that had started in peace and ended in murder.

When I made no answer, Jarris tried again. "What is it that makes you think it's your fault? If anything, it's mine for insisting we go there."

"No, it's not."

I pulled myself up onto my horse, positioning it between Otho's and Jarris' because if Otho rode next to Jarris they would argue the entire day about meaningless things such as the most preferrable weather to hunt in, and I was tired of listening to them. Once mounted, Jarris leaned forward, rummaging in one of his saddlebags for something.

"Here," he said, holding out an oblong object wrapped in a woolen cloth. "This is for you."

I took it from him with a curious look and unwrapped the cloth to reveal the gift inside. It was a simple, unmarked sheath with a long dagger inside. A strip of soft leather was wrapped around the handle. I wrapped my fingers around the leather hold and slid the knife free.

And almost dropped it.

The blade was as black as obsidian, identical in color to the blade Borssa had used on my hand for the blood ritual. Chilling fingers of anxiety crawled up my back and sent a shiver through me. Beside me, I heard Otho draw in a sharp breath and knew he remembered it too.

"What is it?"

Jarris smiled a little in confusion. "It's a knife."

"No, I mean, why does it look like this?"

"It's forged with firedust. Orle gave me three while I was waiting for you to come back down. And I told you I'd give you one, so there it is. Now if we run into Outlanders, we can kill them ourselves instead of running away."

Unable to look at the blade any longer, I returned it to its scabbard. Murmuring my thanks, I stole a glance at Otho and found his face startlingly pale. The sight of the knife had shaken him more than it had me.

"What's wrong?" Jarris asked and I hated myself for the disappointment in his voice.

"It looks just like the knife Borssa used for the blood ritual," Otho answered for me, looking away from both of us as he spoke.

Jarris frowned. "Really?"

I nodded. "I just wasn't expecting it. That's all." I managed an actual smile. "Thank you. Really. It'll be nice to actually be able to kill those things. And maybe you can teach me how to use it."

My words seemed to mollify Jarris' disappointment. Father had never given much thought or effort into teaching me or having me taught most of the skills that all the other boys in a tribe learned. It was a waste of time, he said, when I was clearly meant for other things than stabbing animals.

"Maybe we shouldn't go to the Iron Towers," I said when we were well on our way for the day. Jarris only sighed, so I pressed on. "It's warm enough now, Father's probably already left them for the plains. If we go to the Iron Towers, we'll likely miss them."

"They won't have gone anywhere at all. Not if Gorrin reached them."

"Father wouldn't miss following the herds..."

"He would if he knew the rumors about a breach were true."

"We still shouldn't go," Otho said, turning his head to look back at the plains stretched out behind us. "If they find out about Kor..."

"Stop. Both of you." Jarris made no effort to conceal his growing frustration. "What else do you suggest we do? Would you really rather we wander the plains, knowing that there are Outlanders loose on them?"

I dropped my gaze and swallowed back the cold, sick feeling that wriggled its way inside me as I recalled the one vision I'd had about the Iron Towers. I tried to remember only what I'd seen when I walked Mother's time. The time walking had shown me that they had wintered peacefully within the borders of the Iron Towers, the same as every year. But that did nothing to calm my worry as I followed Jarris' guidance closer to them.

"Yes, I would," Otho said.

Rather than answer, Jarris spurred his horse into a canter.

~ ~ ~

The carcass was only hours old when we found it.

If it had been summer and the grass had been at its full height, we might have missed it altogether. It was nothing more than a pile of bloody bones with scraggly tufts of fur scattered around. No flesh remained. Smears of drying blood stained the white bones and great gashes showed where some beast had gnawed away at them. By its skull, it had been a horse only a few hours before.

My own horse shied from the remains, pinning her ears back against her head as she let out a nervous snort. She danced backward on trembling legs and no amount of urging on my part could force her to take a step nearer. Although they were steadier than mine, neither Otho nor Jarris' horse seemed inclined to get close either.

Jarris' feet hit the ground even before his horse had come to a full stop. He knelt near enough to the pile of bones to touch it and rested a hand lightly on the ground.

All around him, strange tracks cluttered the ground. Tracks that didn't belong to the great cats that hunted the plains. Whatever had made the kill had three enormous claws on each of its feet, large enough to cut deep gouges in the earth with every step.

"It's not near us, whatever it was," Jarris said, looking around. He pointed to a line of tracks leading away. The weight of the beast had crushed the new, spring grass beneath its feet with each step, making it easy to see which direction it had headed in. "It's heading away from where we need to go, at least."

"It was an Outlander, wasn't it?" Otho asked, joining Jarris on the ground.

For all his insistence that he could take care of himself, Otho had made no effort to go his own way in the almost three weeks we'd spent traveling from Abirell to the Iron Towers. I think he was afraid of surviving on his own in the plains.

I stayed on my skittish horse and fingered the hilt of my new knife, suddenly very grateful for Jarris' thoughtfulness in giving it to me. I'd felt the blood drain from my face the second I saw the tracks. The three claw marks that accompanied each footprint told me exactly which Outland creature it was. I'd watched its kind tear a man apart piece by piece. I'd heard that man's dying screams. I'd heard the wet sound of rending flesh and the crack of crushed bones.

"We should keep going," I said, trying to keep my voice steady, even. Trying to conceal how much terror the memory of that creature aroused in me.

There was a part of Jarris that I would never understand. A part that was born out of his gift. I could see, even as I spoke, that what he wanted was to follow the tracks. He wanted to hunt the Outlander down and kill it himself, just to see if he could. A test of himself against such a monster.

There was some curiosity in his eyes as well. A desire to actually see this beast that had been a distant threat our whole lives. I wondered if I might have shared that curiosity with him if I hadn't been forced to watch Brym use the Outlanders as her instruments of murder. But I had seen that and all of my confidence in Jarris' skill as a fighter wavered at the memory. My brother, as skilled as he was, was no match for such a beast.

"No," I said flatly, not bothering to elaborate.

With a sigh, Jarris rose from the ground and circled the bones, leading his very reluctant horse. He picked one of the largest bones up, one that came from the leg of the horse, and ran his hand across the teeth marks that were cut deep into it. Letting out a low whistle of disbelief, he dropped it back to the ground and squinted up at the dying sun.

"We're not far from the Iron Towers," he said at last. "No more than an hour."

"Which is why we should go now."

Relenting, Jarris mounted his horse again and turned its head toward the south, toward the Iron Towers.

The sun was getting low in the western sky and if we hadn't been so close to the Iron Towers, we likely would have been searching for a place to make camp for the night. Having come across the evidence of another Outlander, I was glad to keep moving.

No more than an hour and I would be home with my family. That thought alone was enough to drive away the worry that came from realizing how close an Outlander was to us. It had been so many months. And there had been so many times during those long months when I was sure I would never see them again.

I passed the time as we rode trying to imagine just what we would find everyone doing. It would be late enough in the day that the fires would be burning, large and bright, and everyone in the tribe would be gathered in clusters around them. Perhaps Father would be telling Ahashi a story that our arrival would interrupt. He wouldn't say much when we stood face to face once more, I was sure of that. And he would not reveal on his face what a relief it was to have me back, but I would know it in the way he would put his hands on my shoulders.

Perhaps Mother would be weaving together reeds from the nearby river to use for the baskets we collected berries and herbs and singing to herself as she did it. Maybe she would be the first to notice our approach. She was often the first to notice things. I could just imagine her voice trailing off as she saw us, as she saw me after so many months. She would put her hand to her mouth the way she always did when something momentous or surprising happened. And she would stand, slowly, in disbelief. I wasn't sure if she would run to greet us or if she would be frozen.

Ahashi would squeal with delight and leap into my arms. Missel would laugh and probably tell some joke about how he always knew I would make it back in one piece. And I would laugh too, because once I was back with them, none of what had happened mattered the same.

The thoughts drove away the fear that the pile of bones had ignited in me. They lightened everything inside me until I thought I could fly.

CHAPTER 18

"WHERE IS EVERYONE?" OTHO pulled his horse to a stop beside me.

I stared at the open field that stretched out before the southern mountains. We'd crossed the wide, slow river that marked the border of the Iron Towers only minutes before, our horses still dripping water from their bellies as they stood.

The field before my eyes ought to have been full of yurts and wagons and lines of horses and campfires and plains people. There ought to have been children playing in the river. There ought to have been the smell of dozens of evening meals cooking over numerous fires. There ought to have been watchmen hailing us upon our approach.

It was empty.

Dotting the bright green grass were charred piles of half burnt wood and ashes, evidence that the place had been inhabited recently. Deep ruts formed in the spring mud showed where heavy wagons had sat. Trampled patches of grass, reduced to mire mostly, told of the horses that had been tied there all winter. But the field was deserted, no sign of any living thing left in it.

"I told you they would have left already," I said, turning to Jarris. "We shouldn't have come."

Jarris didn't answer right away. He was frowning at the sight before us as if he saw something there that both Otho and I had missed. Still silent, he dismounted and led his horse forward, toward the remains of the winter encampments. I exchanged a glance with Otho, who shrugged in return. Neither of us moved to follow my brother in his exploration.

It was in that lapse that I noticed the absence of any of nature's sounds at all. There were no birds singing their evening songs. No crickets chirped in the growing grass. No insects buzzed around us. Not even the faint whisper of wind across the plains disturbed the utter stillness.

Dusk played tricks with my eyes, moving shadows across the grass where there was nothing, hiding the distant iron towers for which the kingdom was named. Jarris was almost lost in the shadows, crouching down to look at something, before he finally turned back and started towards us again.

"They didn't leave," he said in a quiet, subdued voice, staring down at something in his hands. The shadows made it impossible to see what it was he held.

"What do you mean?"

Jarris glanced behind him, through the deepening darkness that he'd just come out of. He ran his tongue over his lips and shook his head a little before shoving whatever object he'd picked up into a saddle bag and mounting his horse once more. His face was pale. Almost as white as the bones we'd come across an hour before.

I'd never seen my oldest brother so shaken before. Not when we were being hunted every night by an Outlander. Not when we'd ridden through the gates of Abirell, leaving part of the city engulfed in flames behind us.

"What did you find?" Otho asked.

"Come on," Jarris said, ignoring his question. "We can't stop here for the night. It's not safe."

"Then where are we going to go?"

Jarris didn't answer.

Even with the falling darkness, it was impossible to miss the scene that lay before us. I wished I could shut my eyes and forever shut out the sight of the dead. The carcass we'd come across an hour before was just a prelude to the carnage that we faced. It seemed like nothing compared to what we rode past. And I couldn't imagine just one creature, even one as ferocious and huge as the one I'd seen before, doing so much damage.

There weren't even bodies left behind, only bones. Gnawed on bones, with great teeth marks gashed into them, so thoroughly stripped of flesh that not even the odious scent of death lingered. No swarms of flies hovered because there was nothing left behind for them to feast on. Any hope of recognizing who lay dead was lost. There would be no reverent burial, no memorial stones stacked above graves to mark those who passed.

A tightness in my chest grew with every reluctant step forward my horse took. A tightness that accompanied an ever-faster heartbeat. My fingers clenched the reins, drenching them in a cold sweat, shaking with the tension that hummed through my body. My horse must have felt something amiss for she started to jump and prance uneasily around the skeletons, and I was far too lost in my own ragged thoughts to try to calm her.

As we rode deeper into the field, past the half-burnt fires and bones and tracks that could only have belonged to Outlanders, I couldn't help but remember my vision from weeks before, the one I'd had as Rensi and I and her father's men had begun our escape.

I'd seen the Outlanders destroying the plains people. I'd seen the Outlanders running free and unchecked through the plains. I'd seen the destruction they wreaked. Entire tribes wiped out beneath the teeth and claws of the beasts.

And I thought we'd stopped it.

Edronn and the others had set fire to the caged army of Outlanders waiting to be unleashed on the unsuspecting plains. They'd burned down half of Dragon's Nest to kill the creatures. Rensi had been horrified at the destruction of Dragon's Nest. I'd been mostly indifferent.

Until now.

I stopped my horse and just sat there, staring at one of the many skeletons that littered the ground around us. Staring at that accusing pile of bones that gleamed a ghastly white in the darkness. Great, black holes in the skull stared back up at me where eyes should have been.

I wondered whose eyes they would have been before they'd been plucked out and devoured with the rest of the person. I wondered what they would have looked like. Would they have been brown like my own or blue like Harysh's? Did those eyes see the creature before it robbed them of sight forever? Or were they too busy running to look behind at what killed them? Now, they were just nothing. Black, empty holes.

And it was because of me.

It was my fault.

Just like Abirell, just like Dragon's Nest.

I'd tried to stop my vision from happening and it had happened all the same.

A lump rose in my throat, stifling each breath I tried to take. In my head, a laughter I was all too familiar with rang out. Even dead, Brym mocked my uselessness, my foolishness. Even dead, she was winning. I'd been a fool to believe her, to believe that there was ever a chance to change fates. Her laughter welled up until it drowned everything else inside me out. I gripped my head in my hands and tried to squeeze the sound of her laughter out. I wanted to scream at her to leave me alone. But she was dead, and it was only in my head that she had any voice left.

"Kor?"

I didn't move, just stared, each breath feeling shorter and shallower than the last. The lump in my throat hurt. The racing of my heart made me dizzy. There was a trinket, glittering in the last bit of light, half trampled into the mud beside the white bones.

From up on my horse, I couldn't make out any of its details, but I stared at it anyway. It belonged to someone. It belonged to what had been a person only a short time before. Perhaps it was a gift they were given, a token of someone's care for them. Perhaps it was a family relic, passed on from one generation to the next. Whatever it was, it lay in the mud, a silent, sparkling testament to a life cut short.

"We need to keep moving, Korris," Jarris said, an edge to his voice unlike any I'd heard from him before. "Now."

Still, I couldn't break the spell that bound me there, my eyes fixed on that silver piece of jewelry. I wondered how many people we'd already ridden past. How many more lay ahead of us? And who were the people we were callously riding past? Surrounded as we were by bones, in darkness and silence, I wondered in that moment if we were the last of the plains people - Jarris and me. If we were the sole survivors of such a devastating catastrophe.

Otho was the nearest to me and he reached down and tugged on my horse's reins, pulling her into a walk beside his own mount.

"Jarris, what if..."

"Stop. Don't do that," Jarris said, guessing at my question but not permitting me to finish it. "We just need to keep going until we reach the Iron Towers. We'll find shelter there."

What he said made sense, only sense didn't matter very much to me in that moment. What mattered was that there were so many people dead, and it was my fault. What mattered was that we might be riding past the remains of our father or mother, or Missel or Ahashi. What mattered was how such a thing had happened at all.

"We can't go to them," Otho said, his voice hushed. "Not with Kor. It was a bad enough idea bringing him this close, but into the Towers? That's asking for trouble."

"We don't exactly have a choice. If we stay out here...," Jarris' voice trailed off as he looked meaningfully around us. He was admitting without words our own helplessness against such destruction. Any desire to hunt down a single Outlander was gone from his eyes now. That was, in some ways, more terrifying than the sight around us. "We'll not tell anyone who you are, Korris."

"What about our blood bond? Queen Cholla forbids those as well."

"Then don't show anyone your hand, either of you."

"And what's your plan if someone happens to see them? Or if Kor has a vision?"

"Do you know what's out here, Otho?" Jarris twisted in his saddle enough to glare at Otho. "Because I do. I can feel them. There are dozens of those monsters and if we don't get to the Towers, we're their next meal. So, what's it to be?"

I only half listened to Otho and Jarris, too occupied with my own thoughts to care very much about Queen Cholla and her hatred for the gifted and blood bonds. When both fell silent again, I ventured to ask a question of my own, one that I ought to have asked Drakkus the first time he'd mentioned it. One that I'd been scared to ask since. One that I needed to ask now.

"What exactly is Fentra's curse?"

In the darkness, I saw both of them turn their heads to look at me and I swallowed hard, afraid all at once of the answer.

I expected Otho to answer me, since his family clearly had some idea of what was going on, but it was Jarris who spoke first.

"Well, for one thing, it's more than just a single curse," he said.

"She cursed Brym," I said carefully. "But that's not it, is it? There was more to it."

"Why does it matter right now?"

Turning my face away from Jarris, I said, "It doesn't. Not really. I was just wondering."

It mattered because of what Rensi had said to me, but I could never say those words aloud to anyone else. I kept them close, tucked away inside a corner of my mind, bringing them up only when disaster struck. I still didn't believe them. I couldn't believe them. But I was beginning to understand why Rensi had spoken them.

I said nothing more as we rode on.

~ ~ ~

Night surrounded us fully when the tall, black outlines of the iron towers appeared in front of us. They rose up from the ground like some giant's fingers, clawing at an offending sky. Where they'd come from and who had built them was a question not even the residents of the towers knew the answer to. They were built with great beams of iron and stones that were taller than a man. The base of them was wide enough to house several tribes but they narrowed as they climbed up the sky.

The closest I'd come to one was the winter my father had arranged for my stay with a southern healer. The man lived in one of the stone houses that were scattered between the towers.

Now, shrouded in the darkness of night except for the light seeping out of windows scattered all the way up the walls, the towers looked like giant sentinels standing in the gap between mountains.

We stopped, all three of us, and just stared up at them for a moment. For as long as I could remember, their black, austere presence had been the symbol of protection between us and the Outlands. They'd offered us shelter every winter.

"We really shouldn't be here," Otho whispered, his voice barely audible despite the silence around us.

"We don't have a choice. It'll be fine. We're nothing more than plains people. There's no reason for anyone to suspect anything different."

As we neared the foot of the closest tower, I hoped Jarris was right.

The base of the tower was sprawling, dwarfing our horses so that they were the size of insects by comparison. The massive doors in the side of the tower were only visible to us thanks to a brazier burning brightly on either side of them and a handful of men gathered around them.

The men wore metal armor as black as the night around us, marking them clearly as Queen Cholla's warriors. Emblazoned on each black breastplate was an intricate red design of what looked like a spider's web.

It was the armor of Queen Cholla's Purge.

The sight of it sent a shiver through me as I remembered the vision I'd had of them sweeping down from the Iron Towers like an avalanche, destroying the tribes, including my family. To seek their protection now went against everything I'd seen in that vision and yet, if what Jarris said was true, we had little choice left to us.

At our approach, a single man stepped out from amongst the others and held up a hand to bid us stop where we were. In his other hand he carried a spear, its iron tip sharp and glinting in the dancing light of the fires behind him. His face was almost hidden by his helm, only his eyes clearly visible.

"Survivors?" he asked.

"Yes," Jarris said. "Are there others?"

The man looked the three of us over. "Some. Why weren't you with them? The rest have been here since yesterday and we found no others alive when we searched."

"We were out scouting when it happened. We weren't with the others."

I lowered my head to hide my shock at the ease with which my brother spun the truth to fit our needs. He'd managed it without lying outright.

The man put a hand to his helm, adjusting it a little, then gestured toward the gate and called to those behind him, "Let them through." He turned back to us. "See you cause no trouble or the queen's hospitality will no longer be yours. Hand the horses over once inside and you'll be shown where to go."

I couldn't help but tip my head back as we passed through the doors, straining for a look at the top of the tower. The doors led us into a tunnel of sorts, lined with torches. It was long enough to fit at least six horses, head to tail, inside and opened to a round yard. Stone covered the ground, making each clop of our horses' hooves loud and jarring against the quiet of the night. At least, it was quiet until we rode out of the tunnel and into the open yard. There, we could hear the soft, muffled hum of many people.

The center of the tower, where we rode into, was hollow all the way up and there were windows on those inner walls as well. Looking up, I could see a circle of starlit sky high above my head. Stone staircases spiraled up the inside of the tower, giving access to doors and balconies.

I shut my eyes at the dizzying sight of the staircases winding up, up, up. They reminded me a little too strongly of Dragon's Nest and the rope ladders. Why anyone would choose to live suspended above the world, I would never understand.

The two men who approached us on the inside did not wear the armor of the queen's warriors. One wore a loose cloth shirt and leather pants, not unlike the ones the plains people wore. The second man, however, was dressed in a long robe of black and crimson, the colors painfully reminiscent of the colors worn by Queen Cholla's Purge. Embroidered in crimson thread across the chest was a design identical to that of the armored men from the gate. The hood of his robe was drawn up, shrouding his face in shadows, and his hands were lost in the deep folds of his robe.

"Survivors?" the robed man asked. His voice lacked all expression, all feeling, making him sound hollow.

"Yes," Jarris said again.

He gestured to the other man. "He will take your horses. And I will take you."

We dismounted and I slipped the thin book Semptius had given me out of my saddle pack and tucked it inside my shirt, feeling an urge to hide it that made little sense considering our reception up to that point. I might have felt like a fool for the caution except that I saw Jarris reach surreptitiously into his own saddle bag and conceal whatever he took out in his pocket.

Chapter 19

Y EYES FOLLOWED THE SWAYING black robes of the man who led us. His footsteps were silent, and he moved with great care and little haste, his head bowed as if in permanent obeisance to some unseen being.

Beside me, Jarris looked distant and troubled, his face still pale. I wanted to ask him what it was he'd taken out of the saddle bag. I was sure it was the same item he'd picked up in the field. On my other side, Otho's eyes never stopped moving, darting about from one thing to another, searching for something. At the same time, he kept his head lowered, his posture hunched over as if he didn't want anyone looking too closely at his face.

The robed man stopped in front of a set of doors. Behind them, I could hear voices, scattered and muffled. He laid one slender and long-fingered hand, laden with several large and weighty looking rings, on the iron ring that pulled the door open. I stared at the rings. Most of them were made of dull, dark iron. The largest of them had an insignia etched into the wide, flat top of it. At a distance, it appeared to be an engraving of a long-legged spider.

"Chance has brought you safely to us and Queen Cholla welcomes you into the Iron Towers," he recited in his bland, empty voice. "All who enter here are under her protection and command."

He swung the door open with surprising ease considering the great bands of iron that held the slabs of wood together.

The room before us stretched on beyond sight, curving with the shape of the tower. And it was full of people. Standing, sitting, lying down. There were people everywhere. Children ran around in rowdy groups, tripping over anyone in their way. Some were sprawled out, attempting to sleep in the company of so many strangers and so much noise. Men and women huddled in groups, either absorbed in some whispered conversation or sharing their despair in silence.

"Bring no trouble within these walls," the robed man went on, his voice droning in my ears, "and no trouble you shall receive."

"Are these all the survivors?" Jarris asked.

The man turned, almost surprised that Jarris had spoken without being asked a question. "These are all the

Fates have brought to us. Seek your loved ones from amongst them, but do not give in to much hope, for the losses suffered by your people were great."

For the first time that I could remember, Jarris' shoulders visibly slumped and he let out a shaky breath as he nodded his understanding of the man's words. Strangely, it was that outward defeat in my eldest brother that bolstered my own shocked numbness. All the fear and trepidation I ought to have felt was buried far beneath a wooden façade that carried me forward.

We stepped through the door and into the great hall full of people. Those nearest us looked up at our entrance, a curious hunger in their eyes. I slipped behind Jarris, content to let him lead the way, although my eyes never stopped moving. They never stopped searching for the familiar faces of Father and Mother and Missel and Ahashi.

Colored leather strips woven into beards or braided hair indicated where one tribe ended, and another began. For the most part, there was no mingling between the tribes. Even in trouble, the age-old boundaries existed between us. I saw none of the bright blue that marked my own tribe.

I recognized the aged elder of the first tribe that had captured me almost two years before. His wizened face wrinkled up further in disgust as he recognized me as well. I suppose I'd given them reason to dislike me. The future I'd told them was nothing more than the first story

I could think of and had no hint of reality in it. Had his been the only hostile expression, I might have thought nothing of it.

But it wasn't.

Other members of his tribe shared his loathing for me. Whispers flew between them, sidelong glares in my direction. I lowered my head and tried to ignore them.

I jumped at a hand on my arm but turned to find it was only Otho. He leaned towards me and whispered, "So much for keeping you a secret."

Biting my lip, I nodded slightly. Since the starving winter, many of the tribes had known about me. Few, or at least I thought only a few, could have recognized the sight of me.

"It's him," I heard a hushed voice say and I knew Otho was right. I heard another voice murmur, "Oracle."

"Liar," I heard the elder say.

What troubled me, though, wasn't their recognition. What troubled me was their reaction. It reminded me too much of my welcome at Dragon's Nest. I hugged my arms against myself and focused only on not stepping on anyone and keeping close to Jarris.

After a few moments, I didn't even need to watch that carefully. People parted before us as if I carried the plague with me. The malevolence of their stares was heavy, crushing. I wanted to ask them what I'd done to make them hate me so from the very first moment. But I lacked the courage to face the answer to that.

I lost track of how far into the room we'd gone before I walked straight into Jarris. He'd stopped so abruptly and I'd been so intent on the ground that I hadn't noticed until I bumped into him.

"Jarris?" I heard my mother's voice before I saw her. Completely hidden behind my taller, broader brother, she did not see me at first, either. I saw her arms as she wrapped them around Jarris, pulling him close to her and I heard her whisper, "Thank the Fates you're still alive. Have you seen..."

Her voice trailed off as she noticed me standing, silent and unmoving, then. Her arms went slack around Jarris, and he stepped back, revealing me fully to her eyes. Tears sprang into her eyes, making them glitter strangely in the firelight of the torches. We stood there, just staring at each other as if reality wasn't enough to convince us that this was true.

In the months that I'd been gone, she hadn't changed much at all and yet she looked different. Her round face was only just beginning to show a few wrinkles. Her brown hair, usually tied back in a simple braid, hung loose and rather tangled over her shoulders. I suspected that between the two of us, the greatest changes were mine.

"Korris," she said and just to hear my name in her voice was enough to reassure me that everything would be alright even if I could not see Father or Missel or

Ahashi anywhere around her. It wasn't anything like I'd imagined it, but it was enough.

She reached out a single hand to rest it on my cheek while I stood rooted to the spot, wholly incapable of moving. Even when she pulled me into her arms, I made no move of my own, remaining as stiff and rigid as if I were made of stone. I'd spent so many months dreaming of this moment, this reunion. It was all I'd wanted from the first moment Drakkus and his men had stolen me away. All I'd longed for. And now that I was face to face with her, I couldn't make myself believe it was anything but a dream still.

I'd done it.

I'd reached the Iron Towers and I'd found my family.

The words were like a second pulse inside me even if I remained frozen on the outside. I was home. And yet, I wasn't. There was an undercurrent of wrongness that I couldn't pull away from.

Her head bent close to mine, her hair tickling the side of my face, and in my ear, I heard her whisper, "You should not have come here."

If I'd felt like I was carved out of stone a moment before, I felt like I was made of ice just then. Everything inside me turned cold at her words and I recoiled from her. My own face did nothing to mask the stabbing pain her words had caused me. They were a knife in my chest, robbing me of breath.

I stumbled back and just stared at her. I couldn't believe what my own mother had just said to me. After all those months, longing and aching to get back to her and my family, just to have her say that.

She didn't let me pull away from her, though. With one look at my devastated face, she shook her head and embraced me once more, drawing me close enough to whisper more words in my ear that went unheard by everyone else. "You're not safe here. That is what I mean."

Before I could respond she put her finger to my lips and shook her head a little. "This place has no secrets," she said, glancing pointedly around at the many eyes fixed on us.

Understanding filled me then and I could forgive the harshness of her first words.

Mostly.

I still wished they'd been anything else. Could she not have welcomed me back before warning me? Could she not have trusted that I already knew how dangerous my situation was?

"Where are the others? Where's Father? And Missel and Ahashi?" I asked, trying to look past her and search for their familiar faces. All I saw were strangers, their eyes fastened on us with all the malice I'd noticed before.

At that, Mother turned to Jarris, worry filling her eyes. Jarris shook his head slightly and pressed his lips together into a thin, hard line.

I watched as he reached into his shirt and pulled out the object he'd taken from the killing field and slipped into his pocket. I recognized it as soon as he held it out and I knew why he hadn't let me see it before.

It was a necklace of thin braided leather dyed bright blue. The blue band was contrasted by a white pendant swinging from the middle of it that was thin and sharp and a little longer than a man's finger.

It was my father's periapt.

~   ~   ~

The walls of the vast hall closed in around us, reminding me of the dark, imprisoning walls of the cavern Brym had chained me inside. We'd only been inside for a few minutes, but already I wanted to flee the place and return to the open air.

"He stayed behind with your father," Mother said quietly, speaking of Missel.

We sat, huddled as close together as we could to avoid the prying ears of the other survivors, listening to every word she spoke as if it was the last we'd ever hear from her.

Somewhere behind us, Otho hung back, unnoticed still by our mother and seemingly happy to keep it that way.

Lying on the floor beside us, Ahashi slept, peacefully unaware of our presence and the news we carried with us. I stared at my little sister's face as I listened to

Mother's words. She'd grown in the months since I'd been taken away. Her face was thinner than it had been, the childish roundness falling away to give her an older look. Dirt smudged her cheeks but in sleep there was no hint of the horror they'd endured just the day before.

"They thought they could fight them. At least long enough to allow us to escape," she said. Glancing down at the periapt Jarris had set in her hands, a shudder ran through her. "They did it, too. At least for some of us. I've never seen anything like it. There were so many of the creatures. So many. And the sounds that came from them."

Her voice trailed off with a catch and she lowered her head and brought a hand up to cover her eyes.

"Queen Cholla's men searched for survivors?" Jarris asked.

Mother nodded, a curtain of light brown hair swaying gently with the motion.

"The men at the gate said they'd found none," he said.

No survivors.

Father's periapt lying on the ground among a pile of bones.

Missel staying behind to help fight.

I drew my knees up to my chest and wrapped my arms around them as tightly as I could, trying to hold myself together while everything around me fell apart.

It wasn't right. None of it was right. I was supposed to come home and find them all well. It was supposed to be a happy time. But now it was all wrong. And all I had left was memories - cold, distant memories of Father and Missel that would never begin to make up for their absence.

Out of all the broken pieces inside of me, one remained whole and untouched. A knot of anger that had grown from the time Drakkus tethered me to him. It grew again in that moment, swelled until it was enough to fill me again.

Drakkus had robbed me of my chance to see my father and my brother again. He hadn't stolen my gift from me, he'd stolen worse - a chance to say goodbye. And that was more unforgivable than the tethering, than the ritual, than his betrayal of my trust. That was more unforgivable than anything Brym had done to me.

The people nearest us did not even have the dignity to pretend not to stare. I shivered a little at the weight of their judgment, believing it to be true. I was the one to blame for their misfortune. I was the one to blame for Father and Missel's deaths.

It was a cruel thing for the Fates to show me the future but allow me no ability to change it. I thought Brym must have lied about the order of visions and the number of them. Or perhaps she'd believed it to be true. She'd been wrong about other things.

Mother clutched the periapt to her chest and held it there for a moment, her eyes shut in sorrow, before holding it out to Jarris. "It's yours now," she said, nearly choking on her words. "Although there are few left of our tribe to lead." She turned to me; her eyes hungry for what I had to say. "You must tell me everything, Korris."

It was a whispered tale, told with furtive glances at those around us.

It was a broken tale, told in pieces.

There was much that I left out, much that I was afraid to say, especially surrounded by prying ears. I told her nothing of the ritual or the blood bond that resulted from it. I told her nothing of the information I'd given Brym about Abirell. I told her nothing of what we'd done to Dragon's Nest. I told her less than I'd told Jarris, which was something I'd never done before.

I caught Jarris' gaze on me, a question in his eyes as he realized how much I was leaving out. With I slight shake of my head, I hoped to silence any input on his part.

My voice trailed off as I ran out of words and the strength to say them. My story was only half told, yet I didn't have the heart to finish. There was an emptiness inside me that consumed every thought, every word, everything. It carved me up from the inside out and I found myself staring past Mother and Jarris, past all the people in that room, past everything real. I was trapped in that hollowness, surrounded by that vacancy. Echoes of memories and visions drifted through that space, each more condemning than the last.

S. T. Hobbs

"Korris?" my mother said, her hand resting on my arm
- a touch of warmth against the cold inside me.

"This is all my fault."

"Don't. Don't say that. I won't let you do that to
yourself."

Since I was not willing to explain the truth, I let her
believe that her pleading succeeded. I fell silent once
more as Jarris at last remembered Otho's presence and
motioned him to join us.

CHAPTER 20

EXHAUSTION WAS A MERCY THAT night. It carried me away to a dreamless, deep sleep. I needed the nothingness that sleep gave me, the thoughtlessness.

I'd taken no further part in the conversation, withdrawing entirely into my own thoughts as Otho was introduced, not as one of my captors or the one who shared a blood bond with me, but as a friend we'd met along the way. Jarris was careful, even as he whispered, to keep any hint of the blood ritual out of the conversation.

I think that need for secrecy was a relief to Otho. It saved him the ordeal that the truth would have put him through. And since we now shared not just the blood bond but the loss and separation of family, I was almost as relieved for him as he was for himself. There was enough trouble that night; we did not need to bring any more than we already had.

They were still talking, Jarris and Mother, when my body decided it no longer had the will or strength to hold itself upright. I laid down on that hard, stone floor and shut my eyes to the fast-dwindling torch light.

Beside me, Ahashi's even, measured breathing made me long for a return to the days when my biggest trouble was staying out of the way of one or two of the older boys in our village who thought it their sole purpose to torment those smaller than themselves.

The others around us had grown bored with their staring and listening in and most were attempting to sleep as well.

When the last torch was extinguished, plunging the room into darkness, I curled up on my side and reached into my pocket. Warm glass met my fingertips, and I slid the dragon's blood vial out, wrapping my hand around it. The warmth was comforting, the pulse radiating from it matching my own heartbeat. A rhythm that lulled my weary mind and ragged heart into drowsiness.

I fell asleep with that vial in my grasp.

I fell asleep and while I slept, I could not feel sorrow or guilt or despair or anger.

I slept so deeply and so peacefully that waking was a cruel surprise when it came many hours later.

Sunlight poured through the numerous, high windows hewn out of the stone walls, drawing me out of my sleep.

There was nothing pleasant about waking up in a room full of more than a hundred people all crammed together in such a tight, closed space. All around me, there was muttering and talking and shifting and stirring. Arguments flared up between people, their raised voices carried across the room for all to hear. The fear that had driven those people into the towers had transformed into something a bit uglier. Irritations abounded. Tempers were short. And everyone in that room was subjected to hearing the heated conflicts.

Blinking against the brightness of the morning sunlight, I lay for some time. There was a weariness inside of me that defied the ministrations of sleep. I'd felt it first the night before, when I'd lost the will to speak any more of my time away from my family. I was tired of being the oracle. I was tired of the burden that never left me. Perhaps it would have left me a mutilated version of myself to have had my gift taken from me, but at that moment I preferred the thought of that. The gift took so much from me that I wasn't sure it wasn't more mutilating having it.

Nearby me, a mother argued with her neighbor, an old man from another tribe, for more space for her children to sit in. Listlessly, I followed their loud voices.

I tucked the warm vial of dragon's blood back into my pocket before pushing myself up off the stone ground. Ahashi still lay asleep, sprawled out with her head resting on Mother's lap.

One glance at my mother and I knew she hadn't slept a bit. Her hand moved absently, stroking Ahashi's long, dark brown hair away from her face. She was staring past everyone, a vacancy in her eyes that told a sad story without words.

A moment passed and then another, and still, she did not move or even seem to be aware of my waking. She grieved, I knew, for the news Jarris had carried with him. She grieved for my father and my brother, and that grief overshadowed any joy she might have had at my return. Coupled with her words, whispered into my ears the night before, it rather shattered the dream of my homecoming that I'd harbored for so long.

It took my shifting to a spot next to her to rouse her from her sorrowful distance. Although her hand continued its mindless stroking of Ahashi's now smoothed hair, her eyes moved to meet mine and she tried to smile. It was but a parody of the real thing, a shadow of true happiness. I wondered if she would ever get the real thing back. I wondered if any of us would.

"Are you glad I've come back?" I asked softly.

It seemed a silly thing to ask my own mother, but I was desperate to hear her say it. To say that, despite all of the horror that surrounded us and despite the sadness that overtook us, she was happy for my return.

Her face fell then, a look of hurt written all over it, and I knew I'd asked the wrong question. "Why would you even ask that? Of course, I'm glad you've come back. I've spent months worrying about you and what would become of you." Her hand paused, hovering over Ahashi's head. She frowned a little, staring down at her lap, lost once more to her own thoughts.

"How long are we going to stay here?" I asked, trying to ignore the keen disappointment I felt from how quickly she'd brushed my question aside.

She sent a quick, darting glance to where Jarris still slept. It was probably the longest my brother had slept since finding me. "It is not my decision to make. It's his."

"How long do you think Queen Cholla will allow us to stay here?"

"Does anyone know what's in the queen's mind?"

She went back to her listless staring, and I left her to it, too disheartened to try to keep up any more conversation. It was nothing like our conversations before – there was a stiltedness that hadn't existed before. So instead, I returned to my previous spot and tried to ignore the hunger that gnawed at my stomach.

~　~　~

It was well past mid-morning when the doors to that great hall were thrown open. We were seated too far back to hear anything, but Mother seemed to already know what it was about. She'd spent the entire morning looking a little lost but with the opening of those doors, some purpose came back to her.

"You must stay here, Korris," she said in that hushed voice of hers that told me she was afraid of what others heard. "I'll bring food back for you. But you must try to stay out of sight."

"It's a little late for that, isn't it?" I asked, my own voice sharper than I intended.

She blinked at me and turned away for a moment. "Just stay here. It's for your own good."

I started to my feet despite her words, only to catch Jarris' eyes and watch him shake his head. Standing there, looking between the two of them, I felt a heat rising in me that I couldn't stop.

"Otho's staying back with you, too," Jarris said before I had time to protest.

I heard Otho's grunt of dissatisfaction from behind me, but he said nothing.

When I sat down again, I folded my arms over my chest and ignored the questioning look my mother gave me. I couldn't have explained to her anyway. Just like Jarris, she felt compelled to keep me safe and it wasn't her care that I resented. It was her complete lack of attention altogether, as if I hadn't been stolen away for months and newly returned to her. That stung more than I thought it would and understanding that it was only because of the news about Father and Missel did nothing to alleviate that sting.

The room emptied out almost entirely, leaving just a few very old and young and Otho and I. The emptiness suited me fine. I sat cross legged on the stone floor, toying with the vial of dragon's blood, trying to calm the surge of anger I'd felt at Mother and Jarris' guardedness over me. They didn't deserve that anger.

We hadn't been left to ourselves for very long before Otho got up and began walking away, toward the back of the room that I had not yet seen. Shoving the vial back into my pocket, I got up and jogged a few steps to catch up to him.

"Where are you going?"

"Somewhere other than in here. I'm bored."

"I'm coming with you, then." I blamed it on our blood bond that the words flew out of my mouth before I had a chance to really consider them.

"Your mother will be upset if you're gone when she comes back."

"That didn't seem to bother you when your family stole me from mine in the first place."

There was something ludicrous about the lack of anger I could summon to accompany my harsh words. If I'd said the same words to Rensi, I would have spat them out with all the fury I could muster. To Otho, though, they were just a simple statement.

He hung his head a little and I noticed that he was rubbing at the scar Borssa's knife had left in his hand. "Come on, then, but be quiet about it."

"You didn't say where we were going?"

"No, I didn't."

My effort to garner that information having failed, I glanced over my shoulder at the near empty room stretching on behind us. The great doors at the entrance were no longer visible, the curve of the tower walls hiding them from sight.

Along the inside wall, which we were staying close to, there were symbols and pictures carved in the stone. Some were almost too faded to see anymore but others appeared to be fresh, the white of the chiseled rock still plainly visible. I studied them as I followed Otho's lead. Whole sections were dedicated to the design of intricate webs and in one or two of these, four spiders were carved clinging to the webs, all facing each other.

Otho stopped at the end of the room in front of a bare stretch of stone wall. I raised an eyebrow when he knelt down and ran his hand across the floor.

With a final glance over his shoulder to make sure we went unnoticed, he lifted a latch I had not noticed before and a square section of the floor opened up, revealing a steep staircase.

"You first," he said, still watching our backs.

I hesitated less than I ought to have.

Instead of thinking of how terrified my mother would be upon returning and finding me gone, I thought of how I didn't need her and Jarris constantly trying to protect me. They seemed to forget the many months away from them that I'd spent and that I was no longer a child. With that thought in mind, I began my descent.

Even after Otho shut the door behind us, there was light. It came from the tunnel that opened up at the foot of the stairs.

"Where, exactly, are you going?" I tried for the third time.

"The library. There's something I want to see."

"Do you know where that is? How?"

He gave me an exasperated look. "I know where it is, or I wouldn't be trying to go there. It's not in this tower but there are tunnels that connect all of the towers."

The tunnel was tall enough that we did not have to stoop and wide enough that we could walk side by side. Its walls were made of small stones that were damp and dark with moisture from the earth.

It smelled alarmingly similar to the caverns in Dragon's Nest.

Lamps hung at intervals along the walls, just far enough apart that shadows formed in the space in between their spheres of light. The floor was laid with the same massive stones that were used in the towers themselves.

"You still didn't say how you knew about this or how you know where the library is."

"I've been here before, Kor, that's how."

I pondered that while he turned us down another tunnel that branched off the first.

"We can't be found down here," he added after a moment. "There'll be trouble if we are."

"You could have mentioned that before I came down."

"It was your idea to come along, not mine. Remember?"

~   ~   ~

Semptius had spoken enviously of the library of Queen Cholla at the Iron Towers. As I stood, surrounded on every side by shelves that reached to the ceiling, each filled and overflowing with books, I understood where his envy came from. There were so many. Thousands. More than any other collection of written works in the world.

I could not read a word of any of them, but if I could, I think it would have taken me a lifetime to read through the entire library. I wondered, as I stood there bedazzled by the sheer quantity of books, if there was anyone who actually had read them all.

I tipped my head back as I took a few more steps into the room. Otho had already disappeared in between two of the shelves, leaving me to gawk by myself.

My hand slid to the pocket where I'd put the book Semptius had gifted me. I pulled it out. Surrounded by so many thick and daunting looking tomes, it seemed a little pathetic and insignificant. But it contained some knowledge Semptius thought I should know. Knowledge I couldn't get to because I'd never learned the magic of reading.

Putting the book back inside my pocket, I followed in Otho's footsteps, hoping to catch up with him before he was too far gone. I found him pulling a particularly thick and dilapidated book out from between the others. A cloud of dust accompanied its release from the crammed shelf. Otho blew another layer of dust off its cover and then wiped it with his sleeve.

"What's that one?" I asked, leaning in to get a closer look.

Otho sat down on the floor, his back against a shelf, and flipped it open. Loose pages slid around, trying to fall out, and he pushed them back into their place as he thumbed through it. He paused, frowning, over one or two pages before moving on, but he didn't answer me.

The air inside the library was dry and smelled of paper, dust, and old leather. Dust had collected over so much of it that it was impossible to move without stirring it up a bit. Cobwebs stretched between shelves, in corners of the room, and anywhere else they could find a foothold.

Although Queen Cholla may have been proud of her library and unwilling to share its contents with anyone else, she didn't appear to spend much time in it herself. No one did. If it hadn't been for the light pouring in through the great window above our heads, the library would have been completely dark and abandoned. What was the point of keeping such a magnificent collection if no one used it?

"This is it," Otho said, after he'd worked his way through most of the book, skimming over each page.

"Fentra's curse. It's what you wanted to know about, isn't it?"

I swallowed hard at his words. Sitting across from him, my back against the opposite shelf, I couldn't see what was on the page. Even if I could have, it wouldn't have done me any good. I opened my mouth, then shut it, then opened it. Try as I might, I could not find the courage within myself to hear it. Nor could I tell him to put it away again and forget all about my question.

Otho didn't leave it up to me, though. He started reading and I had no choice but to listen, holding my breath.

CHAPTER 21

FENTRA'S FIRST CURSE WAS THIS - that her own sister, Brym of Dragon's Nest, would not die, no matter how much she sought death, until the end of the world was seen. That she who sought to see all time would live many lifetimes until she grew weary of the gift of time.

Fentra's second curse was this - that the High King Jurri would outlive all of his blood and only when the last of his line had died and his empire had broken would he die, alone and impoverished, forgotten by all who once knew him.

Fentra's third curse was this - that the lower kings of the gateways would lose the firstborn children of every generation and that the gift of foresight would no longer dwell in the land. That their families would be ever scattered and turned against each other, parent against child, brother against brother.

Fentra's fourth curse was this - that the members of the High Council and all who shared their blood or served them would wander the plains forever, calling no place home. That their names would be forgotten, and they would be known only as the friendless, the wanderers. That they would be condemned forever to search for habitation and find none to welcome them.

Fentra's fifth and final curse was this - that the day would come when the gateways broke open and the end of the world would begin. That war would ravage the lands, and none would be free of its touch. That sorrow and despair would walk the world hand in hand, carrying destruction with them on their path.

"Her final words were, 'Thus shall it be unless the gift of sight returns once more to the line of kings and the Fates walk once more among men. Then all shall be at an end.' At least, that's the version written here," Otho said as he shut the book again. "There're others that differ slightly. But they all end, or they are supposed to end, when the gift..."

"...Returns to the blood of kings."

Otho nodded.

The vial of dragon's blood was in my hand without any memory of taking it out. I curled my fingers around it and ran my thumb over the cuts that decorated the vial. If only it were possible to walk back in time, I thought. I wanted to go back and see why they killed Fentra. I wanted to see why she'd cursed each one as she did.

"Why'd you want to read that?" I asked.

Otho shrugged. "You wanted to know what her curse was. And," he paused and plucked at lingering pieces of dust on the cover of the book, "I wanted you to know what we were trying to stop. Why we did what we did to you."

It was a subject we had all, Jarris included, found easier to ignore than to discuss after that first night outside of Abirell.

"We really didn't mean for any harm to come to you."

"If only that had worked out," I muttered.

I couldn't help but think of that night, and the events that followed. The months I spent in Dragon's Nest. The weeks I'd spent alone, traversing the plains trying to return to my family.

Whatever their intentions were, reality was different, and harm had come. And not just to me. Harm had come to Drakkus and his men, to Dragon's Nest, to Abirell, and now to the plains people. Things that might not have happened if I had been wintering in the Iron Towers with my family.

"I didn't think... I just didn't realize..." Otho kept picking at the dust on the book, his jaw working back and forth. "I didn't know it was like that until Jarris said what he did that night. I never thought of it as being like taking your arm. We just thought that if I had your gift, it would all be over. We thought we could fix everything. And we thought it was worth doing, even if you hated it, because it would save everyone. I guess we were wrong, though. Borssa said your gift should have wanted to come to me, but it didn't. I guess, in the end, we couldn't save anyone."

But I might have – if I hadn't given Brym Abirell. If I hadn't encouraged Edronn and the others to set fire to Dragon's Nest. I might have been able to save everyone, if I'd had any idea at all of what to do.

I opened my hand and let the vial of dragon's blood roll from my palm to my fingertips and back again.

"He wanted to talk to you, you know. When he found out you were in Abirell, too."

"Who?" I asked, although I already knew the answer.

"Father. He said..." Otho's voice faded, and I knew he would not finish. "Would you have talked to him?"

"We should get back," I said, ignoring his last question because I didn't really know the answer. Actually, I did know the answer. And I didn't like it. If I could have, I would have. It was why I'd gone back; I knew.

A sliver of guilt had found its way inside me, and it became harder to ignore with every passing moment. Mother would be frantic and Jarris furious and they would both be right. I shouldn't have gone off. If Father had been there, I wouldn't have. Thinking of him made everything worse, though.

Otho nodded and stood, placing the book back where he'd pulled it out of, nestled between two others.

As I followed him along the shelf, I ran my fingers over the markings written on the spines of each book, feeling the depressions without making sense of them.

~　~　~

I was surprised when Otho opened a door at the top of another steep staircase that led, not back into the room where we'd come from, but into a stable. The horses barely acknowledged our arrival, too interested in the dried grass tossed before them. There were more horses than I thought the stable was meant to house. Every stall was occupied and outside the stalls, horses had been loosely tied in place.

"If we run into anyone, don't talk," Otho said, walking forward with a confidence that I tried to mimic. Anyone who saw him would have thought he belonged. "And just go along with whatever I say."

I shrugged, content to follow those directions. We passed by a trio of horses that looked familiar and I stopped to stroke the neck of the beast that had carried me all the way from Abirell, that had carried me night after night as Jarris and I ran from an Outlander. She turned her head, snuffling my sleeve in search of something better to eat. I rubbed her broad face, my fingers following the blaze of white fur that ran all the way down to her nose.

"You won't get her back," Otho said, noticing that I'd stopped.

"What do you mean?"

"Queen Cholla will no doubt demand to keep them all as payment for the shelter she's given everyone."

I shook my head in disbelief.

"You've never met her, have you?"

"No. But she's given us shelter every winter. Not like this, but still... she's never taken from us."

"I have. Met her." That was all Otho would say about it. It was all he had the chance to say before we opened the stable door and stepped into the bright sunlight that shone down inside the tower.

The courtyard was empty. Otho paused just long enough to determine that before hurrying across the stone surface toward the entrance on the other side. Although it had been night when we'd been led through the doors, I recognized them at once.

In the light of day, though, I realized that they had more of the web-like design carved into them. It was an interesting choice of decoration, to be sure, and I wondered if the queen had some strange fascination with spiders that she included their presence in so many ways.

"You should not be out here," a man's voice arrested our steps as we neared the doors.

Otho and I spun around, searching for the man who spoke. He stepped forward from where he leaned against the wall. It was easy to see how we'd missed his presence before. A gray mottled cloak, the colors and tones identical to the stone wall behind him, covered him from head to toe. Even the hood was pulled far enough over his face to conceal it from any casual observer. The fact that he'd been standing there, watching us since we'd left the stable was a little startling.

"Pardon us, but we meant to return with the others. It was our mistake that we took the wrong door," Otho said, lowering his head.

The man made an impatient gesture toward the correct door and waved us on. The motion upset the careful arrangement of his cloak, though, and in a brief, fleeting glimpse, I saw his face.

It was one I'd seen before.

The man had a thin, white scar running down the length of it, clipping off part of his nose and marring his upper lip. The glimpse was gone before I had time to recoil from it. The man turned away from us and hurried off, his footsteps utterly silent as he went.

"That was...," Otho started to whisper but I shoved past him, anxious to reach the door before that man turned around and came back for us. Otho caught up to me and leaned close to whisper, "That was him. The one from your vision."

"I know."

"He's going to kill someone."

"I know."

"Who?"

"I don't know." I stopped, catching my racing breath before opening the door into the great room that housed all the survivors. There was always that disadvantage to my visions. They rarely made it clear who was in them. "I don't know."

I should have guessed that Jarris would be waiting just on the other side of the door that we hurried through, pacing back and forth the same way the caged Outlander did in Brym's cavern. He snatched me the moment I was through the door, his hands on my arms, and shook me a little.

"Where have you been?"

I shrugged out of his grasp and caught sight of Mother standing just behind him, her face so white and bleak that shame washed over me. I hung my head a little but when I spoke it wasn't shame that came out but anger. "If you'd let me come with you, I wouldn't have gone with Otho. But you didn't want me, remember?"

Mother made a little sound and clamped her hand over her mouth as her eyes filled with tears. I opened my mouth to speak again, to try to say something that wasn't laced with an anger I didn't understand and didn't think I could control.

Jarris gave me no chance to speak again. Grabbing me by the arm, he hauled me straight out of the door I'd just come through. I forgot all about the man with his scar that had accosted Otho and I. Jarris shoved me against the wall, not hard enough to hurt me but certainly hard enough to rattle me.

"What is wrong with you?" he said, his voice quiet and icy. "First with me in Abirell and now here with Mother. How could you say something like that to her? After everything that's happened?"

My breath came in heavy, heaving gasps. I looked down at Jarris' hands pinning me against that stone wall and my heart raced faster. The fact that he was my brother and had never hurt me before did nothing to stop the fear that he was rapidly awakening in me.

"Let me go," I said, trying to hold my voice steady.

"Why did you say that to her?"

"Because it's..."

"Don't you dare say it's true. What is wrong with you?" he asked again, shaking his head. "You've never been like this."

I sagged against the wall, the hammering of my heart growing painful as something inside of me twisted up and constricted. It wasn't just Jarris' hands pinning me against the wall that set my heart to racing.

Jarris was right.

Something was wrong with me.

I'd never been so angry at everyone and everything I touched. There was something wretched and broken inside of me and there had been since the night Drakkus had placed his tether upon me.

Squirming in an effort to free myself from my brother's hold, I only succeeded in making it stronger. His fingers dug into my arms. He was furious with me. I looked up at him and saw the way he tightened his jaw and the color that filled his face. But he was also confused. Almost as confused as I was.

"I want Father," I said, my voice a hollow whisper.

"You think the rest of us don't?"

"It's not the same, Jarris. You know it's not the same." My voice rose as I spoke. I tried to get my hands up enough to push him away from me and failed. "I've lost him longer than you have. I lost him months before you did."

"You're not the only one hurt, Korris," Jarris said. But his grip on my arms softened and I breathed a little easier because of that.

"Let Korris go," my mother said.

She must have slipped quietly out of the door, unnoticed by either Jarris or me. At her words, Jarris released his grip and stepped back, leaving me to face Mother. Her face, that I was so used to seeing cheerful and amiable, was red from crying. The tears had not yet dried on her cheeks.

I looked away, too miserable and wretched to say anything at all. I hated myself for what I'd said to her, and I hated her for thinking that leaving me behind kept me safe. I hated Jarris for being right. Mostly, though, I just hated.

Drakkus and Brym had broken so many pieces off of me that all I had left were the sharp edges and I didn't know how to change that. I'd thought for so long that all

I needed was to get back to my family, to my home. But I was wrong. It didn't fix anything. It couldn't fix anything. And I couldn't bear accepting that.

"Don't," she said, coming towards me.

And then I hated her for not being as angry with me as she had the right to be for what I'd said. Instead, she hugged me. Pulled me close to her as if I hadn't hurt her.

"You're wrong," she whispered in my ear. "It's not that I don't want you. It's only that I want to keep you safe."

"You haven't."

She stepped back, studying me.

"You can't. No one can."

My words only hurt her more, although I hadn't meant them to. She blinked back fresh tears and wiped the old ones away with her hand.

"What's happened to you, Korris?" she asked, her question searching for the same answer as Jarris'.

I wished I could actually answer.

~ ~ ~

Sleep proved as elusive as fog that night, always slipping away from me, leaving me wide awake to face my thoughts. Leaving me awake to hear the sound of quiet crying coming from my mother. Knowing that I was the cause of those tears made my efforts to sleep even more futile. I hadn't meant to hurt her so.

The room wasn't truly quiet. It couldn't be with so many people in it. Children whimpered in their sleep.

Infants fussed and cried. There were those who snored or talked in their sleep. The noise added irritation to my anger, and I blamed it for my alertness.

In the darkness, I slid the vial of dragon's blood out of my pocket and clutched it in my hand, savoring the warmth it gave off. I'd held it just that morning, listening to Otho read from a book, listening to the curses that Fentra had spoken just before her death. Not just one curse but several.

Rensi had said she thought I was Fentra's curse, but I didn't think it was possible. I hadn't made the high king fall. I hadn't destroyed his empire. I hadn't killed all the firstborns of kings. I hadn't sent the high council wandering the plains forever.

But I thought as I lay there that I understood a little of why Fentra had uttered those words that had apparently sent our world hurtling toward its own destruction. If I could have cursed Brym, I think I might have.

I gave up on sleeping entirely and sat up. My eyes had adjusted enough to see that I wasn't the only one not asleep.

Jarris sat only a few feet from me, his knees drawn up and his arms lying across them. He held something in his hands that he turned over again and again although he couldn't possibly have been able to get a good look at it in the darkness.

His attention was so fixated on that object that he didn't notice when I crawled past Ahashi's sleeping form. He didn't notice me at all until I sat next to him.

"It was supposed to go to Missel, you know," he said softly, his anger at me from earlier that day gone. It never lasted long, his anger. "Not me."

I knew then what he held in his hands. Our father's periapt. Despite Jarris being a year older than Missel, he'd never been the one meant to inherit Father's periapt and position. Periapts were never passed to the gifted children of chieftains and kings. If Ahashi had been old enough, it would have gone to her, but she'd only seen five winters.

"I know," I said, because I didn't know what else to say.

"If we'd just come here instead of going to Abirell, I would have at least been here. I could have helped them. I could have..."

"You would have died, Jarris." I drew my knees up to my chest and rested my chin on them, still toying with the periapt I'd unintentionally stolen from Abirell. It was like Jarris to think that he could have fought his way out of the mess we were now in. I knew he couldn't. "I saw it happen. When I was... when Brym... When we were running away from her. I saw it."

"Why didn't you tell me?"

"I thought we'd stopped it. I thought," I paused, twisting my mouth from one side to the other as I worked up the courage to confess what I had yet to tell anyone before. "I thought if we just killed all the Outlanders that Brym had, that we'd stop it."

Jarris held up Father's periapt as if he could actually see it and sighed. "I have no idea what we're going to do. We can't stay here forever, and we can't leave."

"Otho thinks Queen Cholla will keep all our things as payment for the shelter she's given us."

"And you believe him." Jarris was quiet for a moment. "He might be right." I heard the reluctance in his voice at that admittance. He hated the idea that Otho could be right. "But I don't see what we can do about it."

We sat in silence. I wanted to speak again. Just like that night in Abirell, I wanted to tell him I was sorry. And just like that night, the words refused to come. But even if I couldn't tell him what I wanted to, I could offer him something that might make up for earlier that morning.

It meant breaking the promise I'd made to myself the night I killed Brym and left Dragon's Nest behind in a catastrophic blaze. It meant doing something I hated.

"I can walk time for you," I whispered. Although everyone around us appeared to be asleep, I didn't want to risk being overheard. The hostility of the others had not gone away with the passing of hours. "I can see what you should do."

He turned to me. "And does this walking time have the same effect on you as the visions do?"

I grimaced at the memory of when I'd walked time before. "Sort of."

"Then forget it."

It would be a lie to say I wasn't relieved at his refusal.

A shrill howl rose up from somewhere outside the tower, the sound of it ominously familiar to my ears. I shuddered at its nearness, at the hunger in that howl. And I shuddered again when I heard a human voice raised in agony. The cry was cut short. The quiet peace of the night dissolved.

"I wonder how long the Iron Towers can hold them off," Jarris said quietly, although the sound of the beast outside had been loud enough to wake many in the room. He seemed unsurprised at the presence of the Outlander, and I wondered if he'd felt it before it announced its presence with a howl. "Save your strength, Korris. I think you might need it for other things than walking time."

CHAPTER 22

AHASHI'S SCREAM FINISHED THE job of waking everyone in the room. It was high and shrill and made me want to clamp my hands over my ears to stop them from aching at the sound of it. She recognized the howls, too.

I sat still next to Jarris and watched Mother hug Ahashi tight to her chest, clutching her with shaking, white hands. There were others, especially among the children, crying out or screaming in remembered terror. They'd already run once from those creatures of the night and there wasn't a person among them that hadn't lost someone to the Outlanders.

"Do you think they can breach the tower?" Otho asked, his voice so close to me that I jumped a little at the sound of it. I hadn't seen him move to the spot on my other side.

208

"Eventually, yes," Jarris answered. "The queen would never just let them in without a fight, though. They know how to defend against the Outlands. They've been doing it for hundreds of years."

I thought of Abirell and Semptius. They knew how to defend against the Outlands, too. Abirell had still burned, and people had still succumbed to the plague. Knowing how to defend against the Outlands wasn't equal to the act of defense.

Otho was quiet for another moment as a second, far closer howl pierced the air. There were human shouts mingled with the sound. None like the first that had been cut off in death. He waited until the last echoes of it had faded. "This is her most outlying tower."

Jarris leaned forward to look past me to him. "What are you trying to say?"

"It makes sense for her to withdraw her soldiers back to the other towers. They are closer together and their position more defensible because of it. Like you said, she knows how to defend from the Outlands."

"What are you saying?" Jarris repeated.

Otho sighed as if Jarris had asked the most ridiculous question and had somehow missed a very obvious answer. "I'm saying, I don't think she'll defend this tower if it's just us in it."

"But it's not. Her people are here, too."

"Are they?"

"Why would she offer shelter if she only meant to abandon us?"

Another sigh from Otho and he moved closer to lower his voice and still be heard by Jarris and me. "Because that's how she thinks. She probably only offered shelter because she saw that she would benefit from it. We make good bait and buy her own kingdom time. They may be used to defending against the Outlands, but they're not used to defending this side against them."

"No..."

"There's one way to find out."

"And what's that?" I heard suspicion in Jarris' voice.

"Let's see if we're the only ones left inside this tower."

There was a dare in Otho's words, a challenge in his suggestion and I knew without seeing my brother's face that he would not let it pass. Outside, there was a series of howls and animalistic shrieks. Although the night air carried sound far, it sounded as if they were just outside the tower. The human sounds had disappeared entirely.

"Fine," Jarris said, getting to his feet. "Not you."

I was halfway up when I realized he was talking to me. I stood anyway.

A loud snarl came from just on the other side of the outer wall, announcing the nearness of at least one Outlander. My eyes trailed up to the windows high on the wall. Squares of the star filled sky showed through them. Iron bars prevented anyone from climbing into them. I wondered if iron was strong enough against the sort of creatures I'd seen.

At Dragon's Nest they'd surrounded each cage with firedust to prevent the creatures from breaking free. There was no firedust that I could see here to deter them.

"I'm coming with you," I said.

"You used to listen," Jarris muttered. "Let's go."

I was staring still at the window when a dark shape filled it, blotting out the stars with a blackness that seemed to suck everything into itself. A snout like a wolf's, only far larger than any wolf I'd ever seen, pressed between the bars. Teeth, long and sharp and yellow, snapped with savage strength against the bars. The sound of them striking iron rang through the room.

"Jarris." I pointed and he turned.

Claws tore at the stone wall, scraping all the way down and digging at the dirt beneath, the noise of them jarring and painful to listen to. A little further down the wall, the heavy, iron bound doors that we had entered only the night before in hopes of finding safety, rattled as something large pushed against them.

A heavy scent of decaying flesh drifted into the room, transporting my mind back to Brym's cave and my time in Dragon's Nest. I had always assumed the smell came from her but perhaps I was wrong, and she only shared it with the Outlanders.

All around us, people were getting to their feet, their fear almost as heavy a scent as the death that the Outlanders brought with them.

"I think we're out of time," Otho said, eyes wide as he stared at the window. "We need to get out of here."

"She wouldn't abandon one of her towers," Jarris said, although there was doubt in his tone even as he said the words.

As I stood there, I felt a hand slip into mine and squeeze it. Mother, with Ahashi still clinging to her, had come to stand next to me and it was her hand pressing mine in both a need for comfort and an effort to give comfort. The morning's troubles seemed distant just then and any hurt I had caused her was lost in the fear of losing each other forever.

Otho was already moving away. Looking back at us, he said, "You don't know her." Raising his voice above the din of so many people on the verge of panic, he continued, "There's a way to get to the other towers if you want to come."

The rattling of the tower doors grew louder, accompanied by deep, throaty growls. Scratching along the stone walls continued and more than one snout was pushed at the bars, trying to nose their way through. More than one jaw gnashed at the empty air.

The iron bent slowly but it did bend.

I was half running after Otho before my mind caught up with my actions. I heard my mother call my name behind me and heard Jarris tell her to go. There was no one lying on the ground still to trip over but the further we went, the harder the press of the crowd became. Although I doubt many of them had heard Otho's words of another way out, he was leading away from the door and the snarling, howling beasts outside it and that was enough to convince them to follow.

Otho pulled the trapdoor open, revealing the narrow, steep staircase. Rough, frantic hands shoved me aside and I stumbled. More hands pushed at me until I was pressed up against the nearby wall. The furor of the crowd made them ruthless in their efforts to be first down the staircase and first to safety.

All around me, the cries of children who were being knocked out of the way filled the air. Some screamed for their mothers, others simply cried.

Outside there was a crash of splintering wood that could only have been the doors into the tower breaking open. The sound set off a new wave of fear and the crowd became a mob, wild in their lust to survive.

It was too dark to see who had forced their way to the door first. It was too dark to see if Otho still stood there or if he'd already climbed down inside the tunnel. It was too dark to see if Mother and Ahashi and Jarris had reached the door at all or if they were still lost somewhere behind the writhing mass of people trying to squeeze themselves into a space made for just a few.

Too small to hope to make my way through the throng, I crouched against the wall. That spared me the fate of being trampled under the feet of the others. But it didn't spare me the elbows, the flailing hands and arms, the feet crushing my own. The heat and smothering closeness of so many bodies.

I'd thought that few had survived the Outlanders attack outside the towers. Huddled against that wall waiting for them all to pass me by, it seemed as if there were thousands.

The rush and press of people against me left me breathless. I felt a familiar band tightening around my chest and knew that I was heaving for every bit of air I got. My heart pounded hard enough for me to feel the pulse of it inside my head.

The triumphant howls of Outlanders lent a new urgency to those passing me and sent a renewed cry of terror rippling through the human mass.

I clamped my hands over my ears. The pounding of my heart in my head was almost enough to drown out the cacophony around me but it did little to slow or ease my breathing. My chest ached and my head spun from the lack of air.

Another long moment slid away, and I doubled over, my hands moving to my chest. Hugging myself tight. My breath was too ragged, too useless. It was making my head throb.

Still, I felt bodies shoving past me, pressing me deeper into the wall. The stone was rough on my shoulder. It tore through my shirt as I was pushed down a little way and I felt it scratch against my bare skin. An elbow in the darkness collided with my head and slammed it into the abrasive rock. I blinked away the tears that sprung to my eyes at the impact.

Shrieks that almost didn't sound human rang out. Screams of helpless rage as someone was knocked to the ground. The surge of bodies prevented them from rising again. I could only pray to the Fates that it wasn't Mother or Ahashi. But it was someone. And they would be missed by another. And as I clutched my sides and gasped for breath that didn't want to come, I knew that sound would live forever in my memory.

If I survived the night.

"Korris," I heard my mother's voice, shrill with desperation.

I wanted to call out to her, but I couldn't. My tongue was like a piece of wood in my mouth. My mind too full of images of Alkan being torn apart by the same creature that now tore into the tower. My breath too shallow and wispy.

"Korris," she called again.

I lifted my head, only to have it slammed once more into the wall by a hand belonging to one of the few men who had survived the first attack. My movement must have frightened him into thinking I was attempting to get in front of him for his action was quite deliberate and well-aimed.

I met his eyes with my own widening ones. There was more animal in his look than human - a primal savagery that would destroy anything and everything that stood between him and safety. A trickle of warm blood began to run down the side of my face where it had connected with the stone wall, and I reeled with pain.

My mother kept calling my name, but I still could not answer. I crumpled to my knees, dizzy with that last blow. All I wanted was to get away from all of those people. All I wanted was to be able to breathe again and not have it hurt. All I wanted was to wake up and find that it was nothing but a bad dream.

A body tripped over mine and knocked me forward. My hands caught my fall, but they were crushed beneath the tramp of feet because of it. Booted heels ground my fingers into the floor and I felt it in every little bone and tendon. And then those feet landed on me, each one driving sharply into my hunched over body.

Someone, somewhere shouted that the beasts were just outside the door.

All I could think of was Alkan in that cage and the way that beast had toyed with him for so long before killing him.

I didn't want to die.

But I especially didn't want to die like that.

More feet ran and tripped and stumbled over me, kicking me, bruising me, pounding me into the floor. My arms over my head to shield it, I gave up trying to push myself off the ground. There were just too many people.

I was screaming.

At least, my throat was raw and painful enough for me to think that I was screaming. There was no way to know, really, amid all that chaos where every sound came from. My voice was just one among at least a hundred others as I gave myself over fully to the devouring fear that had turned a roomful of sleeping people into a stampede of ruthless, heartless animals bent only on saving themselves.

"Korris."

My mind only barely recognized my own name in its descent into numb terror. Strong hands closed on my arms, and I felt my body lifting away from the stamping feet. I still curled up into myself, too overcome to try to stand.

"Come on, Korris," Jarris said, his face only inches from mine. In his arms, her own wrapped tightly around his neck, was Ahashi. Beside him, and holding me up, stood Otho. "Come on."

"Mother?"

Jarris shook his head. "Already down, I think. Let's go."

Otho dragged me back into the press of the crowd and Jarris followed. It was thinning out. We were among the last. The noise was thinning out, too, and because of that I could hear the clear rattling of the doors at the far end of the room as they were shaken on their hinges.

Icy terror pumped through my blood, freezing my limbs. I would have been rooted to the spot, immobilized by chilling fear, if it had not been for Otho's constant tug on my arm. That propelled me forward and my feet obeyed.

As we neared the door, its warm glow of light illuminating the space around it, a woman with a very young child in her arms began her descent onto the first step.

I watched in helpless horror as the same large man who'd smacked my head against the wall to prevent me from getting in his way, snatched the woman by her hair and yanked her back, throwing her and the young child to the ground.

Jarris was in front of Otho and I before the woman's body hit the floor. Ahashi still clung to him, her face buried in his shoulder, but in his free hand, I saw the gleam of a metal blade. I saw the look on his face, that cold, calculated emptiness. And I saw as his knife flashed, spilling red blood behind it as he gutted the man.

A grunt of surprise turned into a choking gurgle as the man dropped to his knees, his hands trying uselessly to hold his own insides in.

Jarris replaced his knife and held out that same hand to the woman struggling to rise. She did not even pause to thank him but scuttled down the stairs ahead of us, looking afraid that we might try to push her out of the way as well.

There was no one behind us. The woman and her child stumbled down the stairs before us, leaving just the four of us and the disemboweled and dying man.

The man's mouth hung open, blood trailing down his chin like drool. More blood pooled on the stone floor in front of him. Blood and half of his insides that had spilled free despite his efforts to hold them in. His face had lost all color. His eyes had gone dull within those few seconds. He stared at us as we passed him and reached out one imploring hand.

I wanted to pity him.

With a wound such as his, the Outlanders were likely to find him before death did and they would make him wish for death. I met his eyes and knew he knew the same thing.

"Just finish him," I said to Jarris.

My voice was hoarse, my throat screamed raw. My lungs were too empty to put any force behind my words, but I met Jarris' eyes, and I must have been easy to read because he nodded once and finished the job he'd begun.

The same knife drawn across the man's throat and Jarris had brought him within seconds of death. That was all the mercy the man could hope for.

We were only half through the door and down the stairs when a thunderous crash announced the arrival of the Outlanders. They had broken through that final barrier between them and us.

Otho pulled me forward too hard and sent us both tumbling to the floor at the foot of the stairs. Behind us, Jarris shoved Ahashi down the stairs and followed, pulling the door shut behind him.

"There's a bar to latch it," Otho said, lifting himself off the ground where we'd fallen in a tangled heap. "It might buy us some more time."

Jarris grunted a response and pulled the iron bar into place, locking us into the tunnel.

The others had continued their mad rush inside the tunnel. Although we could hear them ahead of us, the only one we could see was the woman and child that Jarris had helped. She was hurrying on, head bent and feet racing.

The same lamps that had burned when Otho and I had snuck through the tunnel only hours before burned still, their light a pleasant relief to the darkness we'd left behind us upstairs.

"This way," Otho said.

My blood was still pumping too hard, my breath still too shallow and painful, to even try to pull free and walk on my own. I knew that once my blood settled and my heart stopped its galloping, my body would ache all over from the beating it had taken. But just then, the pain wasn't present.

Further into the tunnel, soldiers were awaiting us. Beneath their helms it was impossible to tell what they were thinking or if they thought anything at all. Their lips and eyes were all that was visible and those were grim on every one of them. They said nothing to us as we passed, only stood there, waiting. Waiting, I'm sure, to defend the tunnel against the Outlanders intrusion. Waiting to protect the towers Queen Cholla had deemed worthy of protecting.

I wanted to scream at them that we were worth protecting too. Instead, I was as mute as they were. We all were. Words were such tiresome things after what we'd just been through.

CHAPTER 23

THE MURMUR OF VOICES SWELLED as Otho guided us to the end of the tunnel. In all the time that had transpired since Jarris had shut us into the tunnel, we had not spoken. I strained my ears to catch any sound of the Outlanders entering the tunnel, but the only sounds I could hear came from those in front of us.

I think it took us an hour at least to cross underground from one tower to another. The crowd that had plunged headlong into that tunnel was forced by its narrow confines to slow down to little more than a crawl.

We'd caught up with the last of the others by then and they had been just as silent as we were. It was as if we'd spent all our voices, all our energies, all our emotions in that room and had nothing left now.

There were shouts among the voices up ahead of us. I raised dull, burning eyes and saw that those in front were beginning their ascent back into the world above ground.

Then it was our turn and I stopped, staring up at those stone stairs. There were only ten or twelve steps up, but my legs were numb with the sort of weariness that follows a long sprint. They quite suddenly felt as if they each weighed the same as one of the giant stones that formed the walls of the iron towers and the prospect of climbing just those few steps was too daunting.

Stopping just then was a mistake. While I was moving, the pain remained away. The moment I stopped and leaned against the wall of the tunnel, it came over me, breaking like the waves of the sea on my body. My head, my chest, my fingers, my feet. One by one, each part of my body awakened to the pain. I tried to stifle the moan that the pain wrung from me, but my mind was too dull with weariness to put up a fight against anything.

"Just a bit more to go, Korris," Jarris said, his hand resting on my shoulder, pushing me forward.

I looked at his hand. At the blood that had splattered and smeared across it. The blood had dried to a brownish color that reminded me of the rust on iron. It flaked off in the same way, too. I looked at his hand and my stomach gave a wrenching twist.

Shoving away from Jarris and Otho and Ahashi, I bent over and vomited. It burned my raw throat. Left a bitter, vile taste on my tongue. Left me shaking with a sudden

S. T. Hobbs

cold. I brought my arm up and wiped my mouth clean on my sleeve, wishing that I had just a little water to rinse away the taste and residue it had left behind.

Still shaking, I finally climbed those stairs back to the surface of the world.

It was a strange thing climbing those stairs, as if we were leaving one world and passing to another. As if we'd died in a way and had been reborn.

Where there had been chaos, it was replaced with order.

Where there had been terror, it was replaced with calm.

More soldiers - their faces concealed beneath their iron helms, their armor glinting in the light of a hundred burning lamps - met us. They gave no indication that our survival had been a relief or a surprise. They gave no indication of us at all except to stand back out of our way.

The mouth of the tunnel had spit us out into another stone courtyard. It was identical to the one we'd left behind, except that it was bigger. The tower around us, rising to the sky, was taller.

We shuffled past the soldiers and found ourselves face to face with the rest of the survivors. A more disheveled and hopeless group of people, I'm not sure the world had seen. There wasn't one among them that had anything left except what they carried with them through the tunnel.

In the distance, I could hear the roars and howls of the Outlanders inside that other tower. If there had been anyone left inside, it was too late for them. I wondered how long scouring that tower would keep the Outlanders occupied, how long we had before they came to this tower searching for more prey.

I swallowed over and over, my throat dry and tainted with the bitter taste of bile still. In the light of all those lamps, I searched the tear and sweat stained faces that stared back at me. My heart fluttered in my chest as I missed seeing the one person I was looking for. Mother was nowhere amongst the front of the crowd.

Another familiar face was, though.

I wondered how the elder, aged and half-crippled as he was, had managed to stay on his feet in the mad dash to safety. Not only had he got himself through it, but he'd managed to keep his cane with him. It tapped loudly on the stone as he stepped towards me.

It was only Otho's hand still gripping my arm and holding me up that prevented me from retreating back into the cramped confines of the tunnel we had just left. There was hate in the man's eyes. Vicious hate that burned bright. His cheeks, wrinkled many times over, were flushed with that hatred. When he stood less than an arm's length in front of me, he stopped. His bright, burning eyes narrowed and his mouth twisted up.

Otho's grip on my arm tightened and I think he meant to pull me back, but I was too tired and too sore to move.

The old man spat on me. I felt his spittle across my face and any other time I would have recoiled in disgust. Any other time I would have backed away before he'd had the chance. Any other time I would have actually cared. Instead, I just stared at him with dull eyes that longed to close and rest.

"Imposter," he hissed. "Liar. You've brought the wrath of the Fates down upon us all with your pretending. Say you're the oracle, do you? Make up stories about the future? Well, now you've gone and ruined us all. The Fates punish us for your games."

Still, I just stared at him, my mouth gone dry, my tongue turned to dust. Behind me there was the soft, almost inaudible whistle of metal against metal, and I knew Jarris had withdrawn his knife. Beside me, Otho had sucked in a sharp breath and stepped forward as if to put himself between me and the old man.

And I just stood there, mute and dumb, as if I were a statue.

I had lied to that man. I'd spun a fanciful tale of prosperity and pleasure in his tribe's future. I had done so without shame or remorse, more interested in being returned home than protected the trustworthiness of my gift. I'd never thought the day would come when those lies would come back to haunt me.

"Liar," he said again, spitting once more, this time on the ground at my feet. "Tell us more of the goodness that lies before us. Tell us what good fortune awaits us."

Jarris was moving forward, trying to push past me. I was afraid of what he might do. He was in a murderous mood and I was sick of death. Slipping my arm free of Otho's helping grip, I stepped forward first and moved past the old man.

"Liar," he called out after me as I walked, swaying a little, towards the others. "Cursed of the Fates. You bring them down on all our heads." He was speaking to the crowd now. "There goes the cause of all our troubles. The Fates punish us all for his wrongdoing. Cursed. Repent and save us all."

The crowd parted before me as if I were the curse and abomination he proclaimed me. As if I were tainted somehow and that my taint could pass to them. The pain that raged through my body was nothing to the growing coldness that spread through my heart. It shut everything out. Turned me frozen and wooden.

One foot in front of the other. That was all my mind could manage. It couldn't manage their hate. Just one foot in front of the other. One breath followed by another. Over and over again until I suddenly wasn't walking anymore. I'd run into someone who didn't scramble out of my way. Someone who didn't curse me in muttered words.

I ran into Mother.

I must have looked a dreadful sight, for she just took my face in her hands and shook her head slowly as if she could not quite bring herself to believe what her eyes were seeing. Her thumb ran gently over a swollen bruise and brushed away a little of the drying blood that had run down the side of my head. And I stood there, rigid and cold as if I hadn't been desperate to find her among the living.

"I thought I'd lost you all forever," she said quietly, her eyes drifting past me and to the others. "Thank the Fates you are here."

I was tempted to tell her that I thought she'd lost me forever, too. That what stood before her then was not the same son she'd missed months before. I was tempted to tell her that she was probably the only one thanking the Fates for my survival.

Instead, I said nothing.

~   ~   ~

Cool water poured down my face. With nothing better to use, I'd torn off the bottom of the shirt I'd been given in Abirell to replace my old, worn jerkin. Mother used the cloth, soiled as it was, to try to wash some of the grime and blood away. She *tsked* quietly to herself when she saw the bloody cut I'd been given. She winced in sympathy when she touched the swelling bruises around my eye.

I didn't bother to tell her that I was bruised all over from being trampled on. I didn't bother to tell her that my fingers were so swollen and sore from being crushed under the heels of at least twenty people that I could not bear to move them.

Above our heads, the sky hovered in that magical place between night and day. It was no longer black but a softening gray. The stars were disappearing rapidly in that grayness, making way for the sun's arrival. How I longed for it. Because with the coming of the sun, with the ending of the night, we were safe. The Outlanders had no love for the light. When the sun came up, we were safe for at least one more day.

And then what? Would Queen Cholla abandon another tower with us in it? Had we only postponed our deaths by a night or two? I shut the string of dark thoughts that plagued my mind off.

We had not left the courtyard that we'd been dumped in. No one had come to speak to us. The soldiers had ignored our existence. All the bickering from the day and night before had petered out. Most simply sat where they'd come to a stop, not bothering to speak or argue or even complain of our mutual predicament.

We sat a little apart from all the others and although no one said anything about it, I knew Mother and Jarris and Otho were just as conscious of the hostile stares I was receiving as I was.

I leaned against the wall, resting the back of my head on it, and tried to shut everything out. The pain. The animosity. The hopelessness. I didn't see how the Iron

Towers could possibly defend against so many Outlanders.

There was only one amongst that crowd that did not sit quietly, absorbing the shock of the past few hours. It was the elder who'd spit in my face. My eyes followed him wearily as he moved between people, murmuring words to them that I could not hear. I didn't want to hear them. I could guess what it was he said. He was spewing his hatred and accusations toward me, eliciting glares in my direction that must have been quite satisfying for him to see.

"I could stop him," Jarris muttered, his eyes never leaving the elder.

Seated on the ground, he still held Ahashi. He'd tried to pry her clinging arms off his neck, but she remained there, her face buried in his shoulder. I don't think she'd looked up since he'd picked her up in the other tower.

"Like you stopped that man back there?" Otho said.

"He deserved it."

"He wasn't doing anything the rest of us weren't."

Jarris finally tore his eyes away from the old man long enough to give Otho a withering glare. "Before he lost it in another's throat, that man used his knife on three other women who were in his way. Yes, he was doing something the rest of us weren't. And he deserved what happened to him."

Otho's eyebrows drew together, and he scowled at the ground. "Remind me never to make you angry."

"It's a little late for that, don't you think?"

With a shrug, Otho settled back against the wall near me. A mischievous light entered his eyes and he glanced at Jarris. "Since you haven't killed me, no, I don't think it's too late."

Jarris opened his mouth to reply. He changed his mind, shook his head, and smiled a little wryly. It wasn't much of a smile, but it was better than anything I could have managed. And more surprising than his own smile, was the one Otho gave him in return.

The longer I sat, the worse the swelling on my face grew, making any movement or expression painful and stiff. My left eye was almost entirely closed, the skin around it puffy and tender to touch. Blood trickled down, not just from the cut, but from my lips and nose. Mother dabbed it away with the cloth, her eyes full of worry.

As the dawn crept up on us, an air of uneasiness settled over the crowd of us. For two hours, at least, we'd sat in that courtyard, our existence ignored and our survival unacknowledged. The soldiers maintained their aloofness. Not one of them so much as nodded in our direction. We might as well not have existed in their eyes, I think.

In the tower that surrounded us, a hush prevailed. I wondered if the tower was empty of the Iron Towers folk as the previous one had been. I wondered if they'd decided to abandon another tower, and us in it, to the force of the Outlanders. The soldiers' presence contradicted that idea, though.

The sun came up and with nothing better to do, people began to sleep where they sat. The night had been long, its demands strenuous. In the warmth of the morning sun, it was easy to set aside the grip of terror and give into the clutches of exhaustion.

I didn't bother trying to move and find a comfortable position. Such a position did not exist for me then. Every tiny movement reminded me of every foot that tread on me or kicked me. Every breath reminded me that my ribs and stomach were little more than a mass of deep bruises. Shutting my eyes, I tried to rest.

"We can't all fall asleep right now," I heard Otho whisper, probably to Jarris.

I was asleep before I could hear Jarris' response.

Chapter 24

TWO DAYS.

That's how long we sat in that courtyard. There was a well at its center and from that we drew water. For those two days, we had nothing to eat. We had nothing to do but wallow in our misery and loss, and in my case, everyone's hatred.

For two nights, we listened with growing apprehension as the soldiers of the Iron Towers left the relative safety of the tower walls and ventured into the night to hold back the advance of the Outlands.

Fewer returned each morning than left the night before, the empty places in their ranks telling a story all on their own. Each night, the glow from the fires they lit found its way beneath the heavy doors, a pale line of light in the darkness.

For two days, I barely moved from my spot, terrified of what the others might do to me if I dared to venture into their reach. The elder who'd spread his story about me had taken every chance to blame our misfortune upon my lies. An insult to the Fates, he called it. An abomination.

I had nothing to say in my own defense, having lied so thoroughly to the man in the past.

Perhaps the Fates were punishing us for those lies. I'd never given the idea much thought but the more he spoke, the more it made sense. I'd misused the gift they had bestowed on me. Maybe they were a bit vengeful about it.

"I could still shut him up," Jarris offered on that second day when we all sat against the far wall, listening to the elder's latest rant.

"You can't just suggest killing as the solution to everything," Otho said.

"Not to everything. And I didn't say I'd kill him, did I? Just that I could shut him up. I'm sick of listening to him."

"We're all sick of listening to him. It's better that he convinces everyone that Kor's a fraud, though."

"Why?"

Otho glanced up at the walls of the tower.

I followed his eyes to a large window high above our heads on the opposite wall. Heavy, crimson curtains hung inside the window, drawn aside a little to let the daylight in. Outside the window was a small balcony, its railing made of bent and molded iron and looking remarkably like three spiders lined up with their legs meeting each other.

"Because frauds aren't going to catch her attention."

I stared at the window. And said nothing.

In two days, I hadn't spoken once. The effort of forming words, of putting together coherent thoughts and speaking them aloud, was beyond my capability. Beyond the physical pain that lingered from being knocked aside and trampled on, there was a soul deep weariness inside me. Every hour that passed added to it. Even hunger couldn't draw me out of it.

Ahashi leaned against my side, her brown eyes languid with hunger. She had been almost as silent as I. Unlike me, though, she broke that silence every time Jarris and Mother went to fetch water from the well. She always asked the same thing, in the same small voice.

"Are you coming back?"

No amount of reassurance on Mother and Jarris' part could calm the trepidation that clearly held her then. She clung to me when they left, a tremble in her chubby hands that did not stop until they returned again.

"Apparently, neither is an entire courtyard full of people," Jarris muttered. He had one of his smallest knives out, the blade no longer than his finger and almost as narrow. He dragged the tip of it across the stone ground, leaving white dust behind it and dulling the blade. It was such an unusually careless action for him that I knew his mind was far from what his hands were doing.

I tipped my head back and closed my eyes, savoring the warmth the sun had to offer that day. It was the warmth of late spring, promising the heat of summer in the near future. The first summer I had ever known that wouldn't be spent out in the plains.

The glow of the sun was bright behind my closed eyelids and if I could separate myself from the smell of so many crowded together, of the nonstop hum of noise echoing within stone walls, of the bruises and aches that held my body, I could almost imagine myself sitting out on the plains. Of course, there was no green grass brushing against my ankles in the tower. There was no soft wind lifting my hair and tugging gently at my clothes. The absence of those things made imagining a little too hard.

Sleep was easier.

Sleep didn't require thoughts or imagination. It just required me to ignore my surroundings.

A commotion roused me from my dozing, and I opened my eyes to find the others rising to their feet. In front of us, the rest of the crowd was doing the same. Scrambling to their feet, straightening their disheveled clothes, running their hands over tangled hair to smooth it. Trying to return some sense of dignity to themselves that had been lost in those inhuman hours of escape and neglected in the long, despondent hours that followed.

I was slow to my feet, still a little dazed with sleep and lethargic with hunger. Even on my feet, I was too short to see over the crowd to find the cause of their actions. Their backs were to me, giving me a little breathing space from their constant frowns and glares in my direction.

It wasn't until she spoke that I saw the woman on the same balcony I'd noticed earlier. The crimson curtains had been drawn completely aside and out of sight.

In their place was a woman dressed in a long gown, not all that different from the robe worn by the man who'd first greeted us inside that first tower. It was a smoky black with threads of red woven all over in intricate designs. A veil of black lace concealed her face from us and contrasted sharply with the yellow hair that hung over her shoulders and down her back.

She held up a hand to silence an already silent audience. When she spoke, her voice was like silk, soft and cool and fluid, carrying far without being loud.

"By the mercy of Chance, you all are saved," she said and paused.

"It wasn't Chance that saved us, it was me," Otho muttered, near enough to me that I think I was the only one who heard.

I glanced at him without turning my head and caught the dark scowl on his face. His head was bent, his eyes not on the woman standing above us but rather on his own feet.

"Praise be to the Fates for your survival. As Queen of the Iron Towers, I welcome you and offer my sympathy for the losses these last few days have imposed upon you. You are guests of the Iron Towers and shall be afforded all the comfort and care and protection that the Iron Towers has to offer."

"Except for the other night," Otho said under his breath.

Her pause was longer that time and she turned her head from side to side as if scanning the group of us.

"All that we ask in return is for your cooperation in facing this threat from the Outlands. My view, and the view of my people, regarding the," she paused again, choosing her words with great care, "the gifted is no secret. However, I believe the time has come that our personal beliefs must be set aside for our preservation. No doubt you have heard the battles waged between my warriors and those demons from the Outlands. I had hoped that such a battle alone would be sufficient to drive back the threat that looms over us. However, it appears as if the breach at Dragon's Nest was greater than King Mitkas of Ludys revealed to us."

Not so much as a breath could be heard in the pause that followed as Queen Cholla lowered her head in practiced distress.

"I fear our only hope is to track the beasts down and destroy them before they breach any of our towers."

Queen Cholla's memory must have suffered some lapse for she seemed to forget entirely in that moment the fall of her most outlying tower. There was a disgruntled murmur through the crowd at her last words, evidence that they were all too well aware of how she'd abandoned us before.

"And it is for that reason that I ask for your cooperation. The Iron Towers has no citizens gifted with the ability to track. I ask, as both Queen of these lands and true friend to the tribes of the plains, that you assist my warriors. If there be any among you so gifted, your services will be well rewarded in this work and the lives of your loved ones treasured above all others until your safe return. Any who wishes to volunteer for such service will be treated as one of my own warriors. It is my earnest prayer that there are those among you who wish to end this incursion and who will volunteer their help in this matter."

The silence continued even after Queen Cholla retreated back behind the curtains that separated her from us. And then it broke. Murmurs of conversations drifted across the stone courtyard. There was a shuffling around as we returned to our places to consider the queen's words.

My eyes caught Jarris' gaze briefly and I could see at once that he was considering her words. I just shook my head, as if that alone would be sufficient to dissuade him.

It wasn't.

No sooner had we settled back into our spot along the wall then Jarris said, "I ought to go."

"You can't," Mother said before the words were fully out of his mouth. I felt as sick at the idea as she looked. "There are others who can."

"Not that many others." Jarris glanced over his shoulder to indicate the crowd beyond us. "And none that stand as good a chance as I do."

"As good a chance to what? Die? Think Jarris. I've already lost your father and your brother. I can't lose you, too."

"She is right, though. If we can hunt them down and kill them before they kill us, we might someday be able to return to some sort of normal life in the plains. Otherwise, we're just here. We don't belong here. We have no real place here. There's no future in just sitting here waiting for someone else to fight our battles for us. And eventually, they will breach this tower, too. Unless we're able to stop them first."

"You don't actually believe her, do you?" Otho asked.

"What she did, abandoning us the other night, wasn't right. But what she said today makes sense. You said yourself that she'll do whatever it takes to defend her people. She must know it is only a matter of time before the Outlanders overrun all her towers."

"Yes but," Otho frowned, "working with gifted? She hates you all. More than anything. You stand for everything she believes is wrong."

Jarris gave Otho an odd look, studying him. "You seem to know an awful lot about Queen Cholla and the Iron Towers."

Otho merely rolled his eyes and shrugged, leaning back against the wall, and shutting his eyes. "Someday, you're going to die trusting the wrong person."

"At least I won't have died a thief."

At that, Otho winced a little and lowered his head.

"Otho's right. You can't trust her," Mother said. "But even if you could, I don't want you to. I can't lose you, too."

With a small, tight smile, Jarris said, "You won't lose me."

Through all their argument I remained silent. I knew no words of mine would change Jarris' mind, although I desperately wished it could be changed. I didn't dare let my own mind wander to what it would be like with him gone.

Ahashi had been as quiet as I through their conversation. With her fingers rubbing a worn fold of her shirt, she crawled onto Jarris' lap and laid her head against his chest.

Nearby, a door creaked open and four people stepped outside. All four were clad in the robes of black and crimson that seemed to mark them as servants of the queen. In the arms of two of them were great baskets laden with golden brown loaves of bread. Carried between the other two, swinging gently with each step they took, was an enormous black pot. It looked almost identical to the one I'd seen Rayka standing over so many mornings and evenings.

The smell of the bread overpowered everything and made my mouth water for its taste. For the first time in two days, something inside of me felt alive, kindled to life by the promise of food.

One of the men who helped carry the pot was the same one that had shown Otho, Jarris and I to the room we'd first sheltered in. His voice, as empty and monotonous as before, didn't need to be raised. We were all too eager for the food to drown him out with our own chatter. He recited a second speech of welcome, mimicking the queen's and bade us form a line to receive our meal.

It went without saying that we were to be the last in that line. And even then, I was shoved once or twice by people who clearly meant to punish me in their own way for what they saw as being my fault.

~ ~ ~

I'd licked the last crumb of bread from my hand, scraped the last broth from my bowl, when an armored man stepped through the same door the other four had retreated into after serving us. His helm hid his face, but I thought he might have been the same man who'd questioned us at the gate and who'd allowed us inside.

In his hand he held a parchment. He made a great show of unrolling the thick, yellow paper and holding it out at arm's length.

"Queen Cholla of the Iron Towers has put forth a request for all those gifted in the skill of tracking to aid in our fight against the Outlanders. Any who wish to answer that call may do so now as we prepare to move out against our enemy."

It seemed a little silly to have gone through all the trouble of writing those two sentences down on paper that he must have known none of us could read. Still, he gave the parchment a little shake before rolling it back up and tying it shut with a thin leather thong. He tucked the scroll under his arm and stood, waiting.

There was a slight shifting of bodies in the crowd as two or three others made their way to the warrior's side. There was an older man among them, his hair already graying. There was a young woman who could only have been a year or two older than Jarris. I recognized her as belonging to another of the four tribes responsible for capturing me for my gift. Another man, his face too weathered to guess at how many winters he'd seen, stepped out as well.

Then there was Jarris.

S. T. Hobbs

All the arguments in the world would not persuade him to stay behind when he had the chance to become the hunter and not the hunted. I had never understood that part of my brother.

Until that moment.

As I stared at him, my throat too dry to speak, I understood exactly why he wanted to go. He wanted, needed, that measure of control over his fate. He could never just sit idle and let life carry him where it would. It wasn't about the hunt. It was about the choice.

And I, who had exercised so little choice in my own life, envied him that. I envied him even as I wished he would, just once, ignore that urge to take life by the hand and lead it instead of just following it. Because as much as he needed his choices, I needed him. His protection and his steadfastness.

"Are you coming back?" Ahashi asked, the same quiver in her voice that always accompanied that question.

The events of the past few days had probably had the greatest effect on her. Not once since my return had I seen her smile. Not once had I heard her laugh. And those had both been very frequent things for her before.

Jarris knelt in front of her and smiled at her. "Of course, I'm coming back. And when I come back, we won't have to stay here anymore. We can go back home, and you'll be able to run and play and not be afraid anymore."

Home was a strange word to those of us who dwelled in the plains.

It wasn't a single place. It wasn't a tower of iron and stone. It wasn't a wooden city set against the backdrop of the sea. It wasn't a city wrapped up in a white wall. It wasn't the high caves and caverns of the mountains. It was blue skies that stretched from one end of the horizon to the other. It was green grass as far as the eye could see. It was the campfires we gathered around each night, the herds we followed.

Home wasn't a single place, but I missed it all the same.

With the simplicity of a five-year-old, Ahashi believed every word Jarris said. She stared with solemn, unblinking eyes at him as he spoke. And when he was finished speaking, she wrapped her arms around his neck, nearly pulling him over. "I want to go home."

"I'll take you there myself, just as soon as it's safe."

When he turned to me, I wanted to ask the same thing Ahashi had. Except, I already knew I wouldn't believe his words.

Jarris put his hand on my shoulder and leaned close enough to whisper, "You have a knife, Korris. Don't be afraid to use it. You have to survive."

No goodbye.

No reassurance that everything would work out well.

Not even a command to look after Mother and Ahashi. Just that single admonition.

Survive.

I swallowed my own trepidation and nodded.

"You have to survive, too," I said.

Jarris' smile then came from all of his victories, full of the confidence each one of them had given him. I expected him to say something about how there was no way an Outlander could get the best of him. Instead, he said, "The world won't be any different if I don't."

He left me before I could react.

Chapter 25

"WHY DON'T YOU JUST LOOK into his future?" Otho said. "Then you'll know if he's alright."

I gave him a wary look. "How did you know I could do that?"

"All that time you spent in Brym's future wasn't a vision. That was you walking time." He shrugged. "I didn't know it was supposed to be a secret."

Settled back against the wall, I only half considered Otho's words. The crowd in front of us was too tense, too on edge.

Without Jarris' presence, I suddenly felt quite small and vulnerable. The elder who'd spoken so loudly against me in the past two days was oddly quiet, sitting with three of the surviving men in a huddle for the remainder of the afternoon.

"Can you do that?" Mother asked from where she sat on my other side. There was a hunger in her eyes that belied her quiet, restrained tone. "Can you really see his future and see if he stays safe?"

I nodded, chewing on my lip as the elder and the three men turned their full attention on me. Their gazes made me squirm a little, conscious of how fast the sun was sinking and how little protection I now had.

"Korris, I would never ask you..."

"I don't think it's a good idea," I said. The last thing I wanted to do was walk time and watch my older brother die. I wasn't sure I could bear that.

Mother gave me a sad smile and nodded her acceptance. Neither of which could hide her disappointment or stop the guilt that needled its way inside my head. I'd given my gift to those I'd hated but I couldn't bring myself to use it for Mother. Something really was terribly wrong with me, I decided. But I still didn't agree to do it.

"He shouldn't have gone," Otho said.

I shut my eyes to make staying silent easier. Jarris shouldn't have gone and left us behind. But I couldn't be angry with him for doing so. He was doing what he knew best, protecting us in a way he understood. I wished I had half his courage. Mine was diminishing rapidly beneath the withering stares of the elder and his companions and the growing darkness.

248

Otho, sitting beside me, was just as conscious of those stares as I was. Without turning my head, I knew he was eyeing me and that he wanted to speak. Whatever he wanted to say troubled him enough that he didn't simply blurt the words out and that left me to imagine what they might be. Since he knew I could walk time, I thought that perhaps he meant to ask me to walk Drakkus' or Rayka's to see if they had survived the plague in Abirell. It was the sort of request anyone would have made, though it surprised me he hadn't made it sooner. Perhaps he'd been afraid to with Jarris around.

When evening came and we were given food once more, Otho still hadn't said anything more. I picked at the bread, dipping it in the thin broth, keeping an eye on the others huddled in their groups in front of us.

The elder was back to moving between the groups, flailing his arms and cane in wild gesticulations as he expounded upon the menace I was. I could hardly blame the crowd for believing him when he spoke. He'd almost convinced me that our demise was the result of my lies.

"Does he really believe you're not the oracle?" Otho asked in a hushed voice.

I stared at him for a moment, trying to decide if I wanted to actually put the effort into speaking. "You didn't."

Otho flushed, the red traveling all the way up to his ears. "That was different."

S. T. Hobbs

Turning to look at him fully, I raised a questioning eyebrow. "How?"

"You lied to us that night about the vision you'd had. You made up a story for Ren."

I shrugged. "I lied to him, too. The only difference is that I never went back and told him the truth."

"You didn't tell..."

"I told your father." I'd told Drakkus more than just the vision of my family dying at the hands of Queen Cholla's Purge. I'd also told him about the world ending vision.

"I believe you now," Otho said.

And despite everything, I rolled my eyes and managed half a smile. "And when did you decide that?"

I expected him to say that he was convinced the night of the ritual when every vision I'd ever had flooded through him. Instead, he said, "That day in the woods. You had to have either been completely mad or actually having a vision to act the way you did then."

The memory of that day made my face hot with embarrassment.

~   ~   ~

Night seemed to fall faster than usual, the shadows coming before I was ready to face them and what they might hold. I promised myself I wouldn't sleep. I promised myself that as I closed my fist around the hilt of the knife Jarris had given me. The ones Rensi had given me were a bit longer, but I wanted Jarris' gift in my hand that night for no other reason than that there was comfort in it.

In my other hand, warm and comforting as it had been since the first time I held it in my hand, lay the vial of dragon's blood. The glass pressed into the palm of my hand, and I dug my fingertips into the various cuts that decorated the outside.

I promised myself I wouldn't sleep but night came, and my eyes grew heavy. With a yawn, I shifted, trying to keep myself awake with the slight movement.

The courtyard was as quiet as could be expected with so many people sleeping in it. The thickness of the tower around us prevented the usual night medley of crickets and owls and nighthawks. Instead, there was the heavy, rhythmic breathing of more than a hundred people. Snores ranging from soft to obnoxiously loud. Mutterings and murmurings.

My eyes began to fall shut and I slapped the side of my face lightly to force them open again. The slap, light as it had been, made me wince. Most of my face was still bruised and sore from the stampede of desperate people who had tramped across it in their haste to reach safety.

In the pale light of the half-moon, I could see Mother, with Ahashi nestled against her, laying down asleep. Beside me, Otho's chin had fallen to his chest as he sat against the wall. There didn't seem to be a person still awake in the courtyard except myself. I wondered if my fears were worth the exhaustion.

Whether they were or not, as the moon continued its nightly march across the sky, I found it impossible to stay alert. Although not fully asleep, I certainly wasn't aware of anything except a desperate need for sleep. My fingers had gone slack around the hilt of the knife, nearly falling off altogether. My head nodded forward.

There was no movement in the courtyard to disturb me. No movement to threaten me. My eyes burned from staying open so long and I shut them for just a moment to rest them.

I woke to a savage pain in the back of my head as it was slammed back against the wall and the taste of sweaty skin on my tongue.

A scream rose in my throat but found no escape from under the smothering hand that covered my nose and mouth. The hand pressed down hard. It made it impossible for me to draw breath as I was dragged, thrashing and kicking, from my spot along the wall. My knees scraped the ground, tearing through my pants and cutting into my skin as I was pulled out to the center of the courtyard and thrown face first onto the ground.

The light of the moon was enough to see the elder's face hovering above me when I tried to sit up. A booted foot on my back prevented me but at least the hand was gone from my mouth, and I was free to breathe. Not that

I could draw any breath past the panic that raced through me.

"Stop," I heard my mother scream behind me. I could hear the sounds of a scuffle and guessed that the others were being held back. "Leave him be."

The elder bent down, leaning on his cane. In his hand, a knife caught the moon's light and glittered. The man stepping on my back caught hold of my arms and pinned them behind me.

"Liar," the elder repeated his accusation from two days before. "You taunted the Fates and punished us all. Perhaps this punishment will end if we return you to the Fates."

Every sight, every sound, everything faded away as I stared at the knife coming nearer and nearer to my throat. I knew my mother was screaming my name, but I couldn't really hear it. I knew that all around me, the others had crowded and that they had taken up a quiet chant for my death, but I didn't notice them.

The man behind me shifted his hold on my wrists and, with a fistful of my hair, forced my head up. The air on my exposed throat was cold and sent a chill through me.

"Stop." I did not recognize the husky whisper as being my own at first. "I did lie."

The elder paused and raised his hands in triumph, a wild light in his eyes. "He confesses."

"I did lie. But not like you think. Not about being the oracle."

Only those standing right next to where I lay pressed into the stone could hear my words. The words seemed to have no effect upon them. They continued their cries for my death.

Only the elder took notice and since he held the knife, terror for my life drove me on.

"I am the oracle. I can prove it. What I told you that night wasn't true."

"You lied to us all and invited the wrath of the Fates with that lie."

"You stole me." The man holding me down loosened his hold ever so slightly and I stopped to draw in a deep breath. "You stole me, and I told you lies so that you'd let me go again. But I can tell you the truth this time. I can tell you your future. I can tell the future of anyone in here."

The elder's eyes narrowed, and he jerked his chin up. My arms still held behind me, I was hauled up to my knees. I stared at the elder and he stared back at me – a silent war between just the two of us in a crowd of people.

"Do it." I let out a breath of relief. "And if you fail, they die," he pointed, and the crowd parted enough to let me see Mother and Otho and Ahashi all pinned against the wall.

Jarris shouldn't have left us.

The thought came bitterly across my mind as I stared up at the elder who demanded my gift once more from me. With that bitterness came an anger that surpassed my terror. I felt it rising inside me like the heat of a raging fire. Jarris shouldn't have left us. And Father and Missel shouldn't have died. And Brym and Rensi and Drakkus shouldn't have used me. And the elder standing in front of me, smug in his confidence that I would fail, shouldn't have tested me.

The heat inside me had to come out. I jerked free of the now loose hold the man had on my arms and glared at the old man in front of me.

"You are going to die," I said, although my voice was hardly my own in its iciness. There was no tremor in it, no uncertainty. It carried with it the weight of too many injustices, too many injuries. It carried all the hate I'd nurtured for so many months. "You will never know safety again. From now until..."

A hush fell over the entire place as my words filtered through them. A hush that I didn't understand until the elder's eyes widened, and he screamed, "Kill them."

There was a commotion behind me, but I was out of my mind with anger then and I could no more stop the flood of it than I could stop the sun from rising.

"You will be hunted from one end of the world to the other until the last..."

The hand over my mouth was less startling than the voice in my ear.

"Stop, Kor, stop," Otho said, holding his hand firmly in place as I fought against him. He was stronger than I, though. "You can't do this. You don't know what you're doing."

Except that I did. As soon as Otho said the words, I knew exactly what I was doing and I wanted to do it.

Ahashi's shriek of terror startled both Otho and I. His hand lifted a little from my mouth and I turned my head enough to see Ahashi thrown over the shoulder of one of the elder's conspirators. What he planned on doing to her, I would never know. But she was scared, and I was sick of it. Sick of the way people used fear to bend me to their will. Something tugged at my insides. Something new and raw and deep.

"STOP," I yelled and as the word left my mouth that tug turned into a tearing deep inside of me. There was a rending pain in me as if someone had taken both my arms and pulled them until my body had torn in two. It sent me falling forward onto my hands and knees. A brilliant burst of pain in my head blinded me. My eyes were open, but I could not see.

Outside of the beating pulse inside my head, there was utter stillness. Not quiet. Stillness. Nothing moved, nothing breathed. There was just nothing. A void of sound. It wasn't hearing something; it was hearing nothing, and I'd never done that before.

"What did you do?" Otho's voice shattered that stillness.

I couldn't move from my hands and knees. My head hung down, the pain still blinding in its fierceness. If pain had an appetite, I thought this particular one must be insatiable. It raced through me with devouring ferocity until my mouth opened in a silent scream and tears burned in my eyes. I didn't know what I'd done but I was sure it was something I wouldn't recover from. In that moment, death seemed like a relief.

And then I was no longer blinded by the pain, although I still could not see. I was lying on my face, panting against the pain that was finally beginning to shrivel up and go away. There was quiet still about me, but it wasn't the same absence of sound as before. That quiet lasted about as long as it took for me to open my eyes. It was destroyed by a rush of running feet and clanging of metal armor.

I tried to push myself off the ground, afraid that the man who'd thrown Ahashi over his shoulder was doing something to hurt her. I fell straight down, my body devoid of any strength. Warm blood flowed from my ears and mouth and nose, just as it had the first time I'd walked time for Brym, only there was more of it. Much more.

A thick rope was forced into my mouth from behind, effectively prohibiting any attempt on my part to speak. It didn't matter because I don't think I could have formed words just then anyway. My arms were wrenched together behind my back and tied with another rope. Once again, the measure seemed pointless. My body had been so thoroughly drained of all its strength by whatever it was I'd done that I was as limp as a blade of grass.

What had I done?

The question was the only coherent thought I had, burning through me as savagely as the pain had only moments before. What had I done?

There were so many people all speaking at once. I heard none of them. It was as if I was underwater, their voices were so muffled and distorted and disconnected. Whatever it was I'd just done had separated me from the world around me. I had the distant awareness that my feet drug against the stone as I was taken somewhere. But I couldn't even collect my thoughts enough to attempt changing that. I couldn't collect my thoughts enough to make myself care. They could have dragged me to the top of the tower and thrown me from it, and I wouldn't have been able to care.

I could see nothing clearly past the bright haze that hung over my eyes. When, in accompaniment to my body's forced movement, that haze flashed into a blinding light, I could see nothing at all. The light faded to blackness and with it, all my senses, only half working anyway, shut down completely.

~   ~   ~

Hands moved along my body. Swift, deft fingers tugging at my clothes, loosening the ties and laces that

258

held them on. I woke to the sensation of being undressed by strange hands. Opening my eyes did nothing.

I could not see.

I tried to shout, to yell, to make any sensible noise at all but the thick rope resting between my teeth reduced all my effort to a single stifled moan. I questioned whether it ever really left my mouth or if the sound of even that moan was trapped inside me.

Cold stone touched my skin as my shirt was pulled off of me. I shivered at its touch or at the hands that were trailing along my body. I wasn't sure which.

It wasn't until I shivered that I realized I had regained the freedom of my arms. I tried to lift them to shove away whoever's hands were on me. They hung limp and useless to my sides as I lay on my back on the floor of some room, completely unresponsive to my efforts.

If I could have forced myself into greater awareness, I would have been panicking. As it was, I only felt a dull sort of horror. My consciousness was trapped inside a body that refused to function.

"Is it true it stopped time?" The woman's voice floated over my head like water. It was familiar and I tried to focus on that voice, tried to recreate the memory that it came from.

"For everyone inside that courtyard, save one." That was a man's voice, also familiar. Infuriatingly so. It teased my mind. My thoughts dissipated like little puffs of smoke.

S. T. Hobbs

I thought perhaps that I was still asleep somehow, that I was trapped in a state of sleep that allowed me only to hear and feel the world around me but nothing more. But if it was sleep, it was the very worst kind for I was fully aware of the pain inside me. It felt as if all of my insides had burst apart.

"Interesting. How fortunate you were near enough to see but not be affected."

The man was nearer to me. His voice came from somewhere just above me. It was his hands I felt removing the last of my clothing, leaving me to shiver naked against the cold floor. And it was his hands that explored my body in a quick, terse manner.

Every touch of his rough, calloused, warm hands against my skin sent shudders of horror through my insides that could not escape. He could have carved me up with a knife and I could not have made one move to stop him.

"Fortunate indeed."

There was a soft rustling sound, almost as if wind were moving gently through the long grass. And then a new hand touched me on my chin. A woman's. The skin of her hand was soft, smooth, uncalloused by labor. She carried with her the scent of flowers, awakening yet another sense in me. The silk of her skirt rested against my arm and side.

"It looks human," she said, turning my head from one side to the other. Bright flashes of light filled my eyes at the forced movement and a sob rose up in my throat, unable to escape.

Inside, I thrashed against the blindness that held me bound. I thrashed against the appalling lack of response in my limbs.

Was it possible for my body to have died without me?

What was it I had done to destroy myself so thoroughly?

I wanted so badly to slap her hand away from me, to slap the man's hand away from me. I wanted so badly to sit up and tell them that I was completely human and no different than they were. But I was held bound by that strange paralysis. A prisoner inside my own body.

"No wonder it slipped inside our defenses so easily," she went on. "Who would have thought the seer would look so normal?"

"Forgive me, Your Majesty, for not noticing sooner. The fault is mine."

"The fault, captain, is with this accursed one. What purpose did it have in coming to us, do you think?"

"You would know better than I, Your Majesty."

The woman made a soft noise of agreement and withdrew her hand from my face, although I could sense that she still knelt beside me.

"It is blood bound," the man said.

His own hand lifted my right one, marred forever by Borssa's knife. He held it suspended in the air, limp and unresponsive to his touch, and the woman traced a finger down the scar.

A strange tingle woke in the scar as she did so and that tingle was a relief because I could feel it, not just on the surface of my skin, but inside me. It was the first sensation that seemed to cross the invisible barrier between body and soul that I'd somehow created.

"Another taint," she murmured. The movement of cloth told me she rose to her feet. The skirt of her garment brushed against my bare shoulder, the fabric light and silky. "At least we've removed some of the other tainted. Bridle it before it returns to consciousness. You said yourself it was moments away from cursing those plains' wretches. I'll have no curses made upon me or my house. Bring it to the hall of Chance once you are through. I cannot risk it's being left alone. Who knows what damage it seeks to cause us."

A protest welled up inside my mind but made it no further. From only a few feet away, a door creaked open and then shut again. The queen retreated in slow, measured steps and another, heavier person entered to take her place.

The one who entered wore at least a few pieces of armor. He clanged and clacked loudly with every step as he crossed the room. His armor creaked and squealed as he knelt at my side.

"Hold him," the captain ordered, and I felt my body shifting in the hands of yet another person.

Sitting me up, they loosened the knot that held the rope in my mouth.

"Can he speak?" the man holding me asked, his voice painfully close to my ear and loud.

"Not yet. He's not come to. Nor will he for many hours."

There was a sigh of relief, the heat of the man's breath brushing against my bare skin. Then the rope was pulled free and for one glorious moment, my mouth was free. There was an ache in my jaw from the thickness of the rope.

I tried to suck in a breath but before I could, cold metal slid between my lips and teeth, coming to rest on my tongue. It was wide and thick and flat, filling my mouth and holding my tongue down, and it belonged to a larger contraption. Unyielding bands of iron closed around my face and head, making it impossible for me to spit out the mouthpiece even if I could have made the effort to do so. One of the bands went up over the top of my head and under my chin, the others wrapped around to the back of my head.

Once fitted on, it forced my teeth together hard, the bit of metal between them the only thing keeping them from grinding against each other.

I heard them lock the device shut behind my head and the iron bands pressed deep into my jaw and the sides of my head and under my chin. It rubbed against the bruises that lingered still.

I made another effort to bring my hands up, more frantic than the first. I could not so much as move my mouth without the metal plate pressing my tongue down and the iron bands chafing against my skull. My arms still refused to obey me, though.

When my captor released his hold on me, I fell back onto the hard floor, the metal of the device digging deep into the back of my head as it struck the ground, letting loose a ringing pain inside my head.

So completely detached from my own body, the pain was simple. It just hurt. And I could not even complain about it.

When my arms were lifted and my body dragged across the floor, my senses deserted me once more.

Chapter 26

"OU'RE MAJESTY, PRINCE OTHO of Ludys requests an audience with you."

The voice was one I'd heard before – it belonged to the man who'd held me still while Queen Cholla's captain bound my head with an iron bridle.

"Prince Otho? I was not aware that he was here in the Iron Towers. What is it he desires to speak to me about?"

"He says that it is for your ears alone."

"Very well, Keis, show him in. And continue your search for the bonded."

"He does not come alone, Your Majesty. There is a woman and child with him that he insists must come too. And he said that our search for the bonded one is no longer needed."

"Does he?" Queen Cholla said, a slight annoyance in her tone. "So be it. I shall see them all."

S. T. Hobbs

Footsteps rang, loud and jarring, across the floor. A door opened and then shut again. The footsteps faded.

"What think you of it?" Queen Cholla asked.

"It draws its kind to us," a bland, empty voice answered. Another voice I'd heard before, coming from a man in black and red robes, guiding Jarris and Otho and I to the hall of survivors. "It calls them forth by its presence."

"You believe its presence is the reason the Outlanders have come?"

My ears were the only part of my body that seemed to work, and I clung to every word, every sound that reached them. Those sounds were my link to the world of the living, all I had left for the time being.

"It drew them first at Dragon's Nest and then at Abirell. Now here. The evidence speaks for itself. Where it goes, the Outlanders follow."

"Hmmm. Perhaps. And now Mitkas has moved to secure Dragon's Nest for himself."

"Your Majesty fears his intentions." The monotone voice did not ask a question. "Abirell is now fallen, and none have moved to secure it."

"Are you suggesting that I bring Abirell under the protection of the Iron Towers?"

"As a servant of Chance, I suggest nothing. I only say what is, not what may or may not be. The path is yours to choose."

266

"Yet I have the distinct impression that you would be pleased by such an action on my part. Come now, Priest of Chance, advise me as you are meant to do. What choices lie before me and what outcomes will they lead to?"

"You know Mitkas to be a threat. Given the opportunity, he will move to take Abirell. If he holds three gateways, he stands one step closer to becoming the high king and we are at his mercy. If the Iron Towers and Abirell stood united against him, his threat is greatly diminished, and the world is balanced once more."

"Would that Drakkus had taken the throne of Ludys instead of Mitkas." Queen Cholla sighed.

"Drakkus sought always to strengthen alliances. Mitkas seeks only the destruction of alliances."

The sound of footsteps grew louder, and the doors opened.

"Prince Otho of Ludys, Your Majesty," Keis' voice announced.

"Prince Otho," Queen Cholla said. "I was unaware of your arrival to the Iron Towers. For what purpose have you come?"

"I've come to tell you that your search for the one who shares a blood bond with the oracle is not necessary. His bond is with me."

Queen Cholla made a little noise of surprise. "And how is it that the prince of Ludys finds himself blood bound to the seer? Was this part of your father's mad scheme?"

"It was my father's attempt to end Fentra's curse, yes."

"A failed attempt, it would seem," Queen Cholla said, musing. "What did he hope to accomplish by creating this blood bond?"

"He thought that if the gift of foresight returned once more to the line of kings, then the curses would be ended. As you say, it was a failed attempt."

"He performed a blood ritual to take that creature's gift," she said, a hint of disgust entering her voice, "and make it yours? I suppose a blood bond was the best outcome that could have come from such an abomination. You are no firstborn of a king, Prince Otho. Your father was mad to think such a trick would work."

The footsteps came closer, crossing the wide-open space of the room. As they neared, there was a horrified gasp.

"What have you done to him?"

My mother's voice jolted me out of the lethargy that held me but still I did not open my eyes. Cowardice kept them shut. Fear that my sight would still be gone.

But even without my eyes open, her sudden presence was enough to force my mind into an exploration of my surroundings that extended past just listening.

I was lying on the floor, my limbs numb and leaden, my senses hazy. It took me a little longer to determine that I was once again clothed and the thought of being dressed by a stranger while I lay unconscious was every bit as disturbing as being undressed by a stranger while awake.

"It seems, Prince Otho, that your time among the plains people has robbed you of the good manners you were brought up on. You have not yet introduced me to those you insisted on bringing into my presence." Queen Cholla said.

"I'm Korris' mother."

"Ah... but I think you are not. Not really."

I waited, unable to move, to speak. Just listening for my mother's denial of the queen's declaration.

It didn't come.

"Please, just let him go. We'll leave the Towers; we'll be gone at once. You'll never have to see us again."

There was a long silence, broken only by the soft padding of footsteps pacing back and forth and the gentle rustle of cloth swaying with each step.

"I cannot release him," Queen Cholla said at last. "Not when he is capable of cursing time or stopping it. He is a menace not fit for the world."

"He's my son. I know him. He would never hurt anyone."

I'd never told her about killing Brym. I'd never told her about when I struck Rensi or how I'd held the knowledge of an attack on Drakkus' camp a secret.

"Prince Otho," Queen Cholla began, ignoring my mother's plea, "you will accompany the high priestess as she searches for a way to rid you of your blood bond. Such an abomination does not belong to a prince."

Otho said nothing in answer to her, but I heard footsteps retreating once more from the room.

"How many winters has your son seen?"

"Fifteen, Your Majesty."

"Hmmm. There is a chance... something we can try."

"Anything, so long as he is spared." I heard the plea in my mother's voice, tears held back by just a thread of control.

"I am a mother, myself. I know what it is to long for your child's wellbeing." Queen Cholla paused. She was fond of those weighty pauses, letting them do half her talking for her. "But he is tainted, and his taint has brought harm to us all. It is possible that my servants of Chance may be able to purge him of that taint. He is young enough yet that the gift may not have settled within him."

"Will he be hurt?"

Queen Cholla did not answer right away. Her silence gave me another moment to try to rouse myself further. The imprisoning grasp of unconsciousness was reluctant to loosen its fingers from my mind but my awareness of my own body and surroundings grew gradually. I could smell the sweet, heavy scent of flowers that accompanied Queen Cholla. It mingled with the acrid smell of incensed smoke.

Closed like a vice around my head, the metal cage that kept my mouth shut dug into my skin. The iron bands that met at the back of my head pressed in deep. The longer I laid there awake, the more desperate my desire to be rid of the thing grew. I brought my hands up, relieved to find that they actually moved at my command again, and clawed at the iron. As frantic as the effort was, I knew before I'd even started that it was useless. Bare hands against iron never win. My fingernails tore into my own skin, though, trying to get underneath the iron.

With my futile fight against my iron gag, I lost the concentration needed to keep my eyes shut. Gray nothingness met me. A muted sound of despair slipped past the bit of metal in my mouth as understanding washed over me. Whatever I'd done in that courtyard had cost me my eyesight and the longer it stayed away the more I despaired of ever getting it back.

Reason abandoned me.

Driven frantic by that blindness and by my enforced silence, I renewed my efforts to free my face and mouth even as I felt warm blood trickling down from where my fingernails dug furrows into my skin. The pain was nothing compared to the horror of being robbed of both my sight and my voice. Tears slid free of my blind eyes, mingling with the blood.

"Korris, stop," my mother said, her voice suddenly quite near me. I felt her hands close over mine, pulling them away from their useless task. "You're hurting yourself."

I was blind.

I was blind. I couldn't see, I couldn't speak. I was so wholly trapped inside myself and I couldn't break out.

My mother's voice assuaged none of my rapidly growing hysteria. Her hands on my own did nothing except add another layer to my imprisonment.

I fought her, pulled against her grip, but I was weak still. My insides felt as if someone had dumped them all out, shaken them around and then returned them with little care for where they went. My limbs weighed as if they were made of iron.

"Korris, please stop," she continued to plead with me. "You're making it worse."

As if it were my fault.

There wasn't anything worse.

There was no way to make anything worse.

I couldn't breathe. Not with my mouth sealed shut. I was suffocating.

And all my mother said was that I was making it worse. Not that she would help me or that she would find a way to get me out of Queen Cholla's grasp. Just that I was making it worse. But I wasn't doing anything except trying to get free and that couldn't have been wrong.

My entire body shook.

My every breath was loud and ragged and harsh. I wanted out of my own darkness, my own silence. My skin underneath the iron bands was hot and damp with sweat and blood and tears as I freed my hands from my mother's and pulled once more at the cage.

There were other hands that stopped me next. A man's hands, large and strong, pulling mine away from my face, pulling them behind me and pinning them there. His hold wasn't meant to inflict more pain on me, but I was beyond caring. I threw myself against his hold and almost wrenched my arms out of place.

"Korris," my mother said, her voice closer, softer than it had been before. Her hands cradled my face, a gentle touch that defied what she was asking of me. "Listen to me. Listen. You have to stop. You can't fight them. You can't. They'll only hurt you if you do." She was whispering then, close to my ear and too quiet for any but myself to hear. "She's going to take your gift, but it will be for the best." A spasm ran through me at her words; another muted, broken sound slipped past the iron bit. "We don't have a choice, Korris. If she takes your gift, you'll survive. And when it is gone, we will be together again. Do you hear me? We'll all be together again, and you'll never have to leave again."

I couldn't breathe.

I couldn't see her face.

I couldn't utter a single word to her.

I couldn't breathe and I was desperate to. My lungs burned for want of air but refused to work properly.

S. T. Hobbs

Tremors rattled my entire body as I writhed in that man's grasp, unable to break free and therefore unable to reach the iron contraption that imprisoned my head and suffocated me.

"Can you not take this off him?"

My mother wasn't speaking to me any longer. But her hands were still on me, cupping my face, a warmth that I leaned against as my body gave up its fight.

"We daren't. I will not provide him opportunity to curse any of us," Queen Cholla said.

"He wouldn't..."

"It was exactly what he was doing to the other survivors. It is not a risk I'm willing to take. No, he will remain bridled and tonight the servants of Chance will begin their purge."

"I'm staying with him."

Queen Cholla's sigh was loud and not entirely without sympathy. "I'm afraid that won't be possible. The purging is not something that can be witnessed."

I heard my mother start to speak but Queen Cholla cut her off. "You will stay near, that is the best I can offer you. I will have a room for you and your daughter to stay in where you will be protected and safe."

"No," I heard my mother's voice sharpen. She pulled away from me and I began to thrash against my captor's grip once more.

"This isn't a discussion. The only choice you have is to leave willingly..."

"How long will it take?"

Queen Cholla sighed again, less with sympathy and more with impatience. "I will send for you as soon as we are through."

I stilled, frozen, listening above the sound of my own harsh breathing. I was listening for my mother to argue further, to insist on staying by my side in whatever future horrors awaited me. If I could have just seen her face, I would have been satisfied.

Instead, I just heard the dismal sound of retreating footsteps.

Chapter 27

I HATED THE COLOR GRAY.

Now it was all I could see. Gray and gray and more gray. There were shades of lighter gray and shades of darker gray, but it was gray all the same.

I hated it.

"Feed him, Keis, and stay within sight of him until I return this evening."

Those were Queen Cholla's parting words before she left me to wallow in a pool of bitter fear.

How many hours had to pass before evening came, I did not know. Nor could I know when all I saw was shades of gray and my only form of communication had been reduced to a nod or shake of my head.

Keis proved to be the man who'd held me while Mother tried to calm my panic. He still had hold of my arms when he began to speak. His voice was too loud for as close as he was to my ear, and I cringed at it and tried once more to pull away from him.

"Before we get on with this, there's something you ought to understand and that's that Her Majesty couldn't care less what becomes of me, so it makes no difference to her if you curse me or not. However, I've got the strictest orders to cut your tongue out if you utter so much as a word when you're given the chance."

His words came quick and sharp, barely giving me space to think between each new statement. There were a thousand questions I had to ask but couldn't.

"You do understand, don't you? I've got to take this off for you to eat but it'll cost you your tongue if you try to speak. So, all you have to do is stay quiet and there will be no trouble at all."

The temptation of food and having a few moments of freedom from the bridling device was enough to make me nod in understanding. The threat of having my tongue removed was enough for me to quench every temptation to yell the moment my mouth was free.

Keis huffed and shifted so that he was no longer behind me, pinning my arms behind my back, but in front of me. His armor creaked and squealed with each little move, a dissonant melody of iron and leather. I was glad of that sound. Blind as I was, that sound meant Keis, at least, couldn't sneak up on me.

"Good, good. You behave yourself and you just might get to return to your family once you've been purged. That is, if the purging works. It don't always."

Those words sent another tremor through me. I had never chosen my gift, but it was mine and not theirs to purge from me.

Keis reached behind my head with a key in his hand. A soft click, and the iron bands released their vice-like grip around my head. It hinged open on either side just in front of my ears and Keis pulled the thing off, taking with it the metal bit from my mouth.

Nothing could ever compare to that first moment of freedom. It was only half freedom at best.

I was still forbidden to speak.

I was still blind.

I was still condemned to a purging that would strip part of myself away.

But I could stretch my aching jaw and fresh air could cool the hot, sweaty skin that had been trapped under metal and my tongue, swollen and parched as it was, could move without pressing against hard metal and my neck was relieved of the constant weight of the cage.

I let my body sink to the floor, savoring how good it felt to lay down without the bridling device. The first twinges of pain as my muscles relaxed a little were not enough to rob the moment of its relief. Keis was almost redeemed from his former actions simply by being the one to give me those few moments of respite.

"Might as well eat while you have the chance. There's no point in keeping you locked up here alive if you're planning on starving yourself to death."

Something slid across the stone floor towards me, and I reached out a groping hand to find it. My fingers met a tray and then a bowl and a piece of bread and then a cup. It was the cup I pulled towards me first, propping myself up on my elbow to drink from it.

A single cupful of water, tasting so strongly of iron that I almost spewed it out, was all I received. My tongue was too swollen to drink it nearly as fast as I would have liked. And when it was gone, I wished I had taken more time with it and relished each sip of it more. It barely touched my thirst, but I did not dare speak to ask for more.

In the bowl was a thick, creamy broth. With Keis' noisy breathing coming from nearby, I tried to devour the hard bread he'd brought but found my jaw too tender to chew it. I dipped it in the broth to soften it, but it still hurt far too much and I eventually had to content myself with picking up the bowl of broth and drinking it.

I was still famished.

Keis kept silent until I'd finished the last drops of broth and had tried once more to eat the bread. When I was finished, I heard him rise, squeaking in his armor.

"Hold still, then," Keis said.

His hand grabbed the back of my head, pulling it toward him. Toward the bridling device.

Although I was forbidden to speak, the desperation that filled me was almost strong enough to ignore Keis' words of warning. I longed to beg him to get the thing as far from me as possible. I would have promised him almost anything in return for that simple freedom. My mouth still tasted the iron. My face still felt its bruising. I wasn't ready to return to the crushing weight and presence of it.

"Now, now. Don't look at me so," Keis said as he knelt before me, his voice almost kind. I was getting sick of kind people doing cruel things all for the sake of a cause they'd deemed right. It made their kindness, when it came, worthless. "You must wear it because Her Majesty orders it so. And don't think you can make me feel sorry enough for you as to disobey her orders."

There was a tremble in my chin that I could not stop. I heard the soft clang of the iron as he brought it to my face and all I could do was shake my head in a mute plea for mercy.

"It don't make it any easier, you putting up a fuss about it."

"Please." The word escaped in a single breath, a whisper I hadn't meant to let out. I gasped in horror at my own failure and waited for Keis to obey his queen's orders.

He'd heard me. I knew he had, for he had gone very still. It was only for a moment and then he was moving again as if nothing had happened, as if I hadn't just disobeyed the single rule he'd given me.

His free hand grabbed my chin and held it firm, preventing me from turning away as he forced the metal bit back between my teeth. As he locked it around my head once more, I made a little sound of despair that could barely be heard.

He let out a little sigh, his breath hot against my skin because he was sitting so close to me.

"It's not the worst thing that's going to happen to you. I'd rest while I could if I was you. The priest and priestess like to do their work in the night hours."

Rest was the farthest thing from my mind and his reminder of what I faced drove it even further away.

~ ~ ~

I hated the color gray.

If voices had colors, then the voice of the man hovering over me was the grayest I'd ever heard. It was the voice of the same man who had guided Jarris, Otho, and I into the room full of survivors only a few short days before. It was the same voice I'd listened to while it discussed my fate with Queen Cholla. It was that same bland, empty voice that neither rose nor fell as it droned on. It was the voice of the high priest of Chance.

For interminable long hours, I hadn't moved. I'd lain, crumpled on the stone floor, my head too heavy to hold up, my body too weak and hurting to try to drag myself away.

I wouldn't have made it far if I had tried.

Keis' loud breathing and louder armor had remained within hearing for all those hours, and it was Keis who, at the end of those hours, had pulled me to my unsteady and uncooperative feet and dragged me across the hall of Chance to a table.

It was that table that I found myself lying on my back on, my hands stretched far above my head and chained along with my feet, with the droning, gray voice of the high priest of Chance filling my ears.

The air around the table was thick and heavy and full of smoke, making every breath a struggle. The smoke burned inside my nose. I couldn't cough, though my lungs were desperate to expel the smoke.

The chains that held me to the table rattled a little with the tremors that wracked my body. I listened to that instead of the gray voice of the high priest. He chanted in a tongue I did not understand, anyway.

My mind drifted on a sea of terror, remembering just what Jarris had said about what it felt like to lose a gift. I wondered how right he was. Would I spend the rest of my life longing for something that I knew was missing? Would it leave me a wreck as he had said? Or would the purging fail entirely and leave me to face whatever Queen Cholla did with unpurged, gifted people?

"It is ready?" Queen Cholla asked.

I started at the sound of her voice so near me. I hadn't heard her approach.

"All is ready. We wait only for you and your flame."

"Very well."

The high priest went back to his chanting, reminding me horribly of Brym and her incessant chants as she stared through her eye of a dragon periapt. I no longer had her periapt, or the one I'd unintentionally stolen from Abirell. They had been taken from me when I was stripped and searched.

All around me, the air grew cold, and a chill ran over my skin. I didn't mean to, but I yanked against the chains holding me down. I couldn't help it. As the droning voice of the high priest continued, a slight change came over it. His words, bland as ever, came faster, clipped off sharper. A second voice joined his - a woman's, just as bland and gray as the high priest's. The staccato of their joint voices sped up again, although they dropped to barely a whisper. Each new, strange word sent another chill through me. Faster and faster their words came, weaving a sinister spell of tension into the smoke-filled air.

A howl pierced the air outside the tower, carried on the cooling wind of the night. It came from some distance, but its hunger was unmistakable. Another howl answered, equal in its hunger but nearer.

"Let's begin before it is too late," Queen Cholla said.

CHAPTER 28

THE CRASH OF A DOOR THROWN open reverberated in the spacious hall of Chance. It interrupted the cadence of the chanting, and I heard a sharp intake of breath. Without my sight, I was left to guess who had been startled by the intrusion.

For my own part, a fleeting moment of relief filled me at the unexpected delay.

"What are you doing to him?"

I'd never thought there would be a time when I was happy to hear Otho's voice but in that moment, I could think of no better sound to my ears. In my head, I knew his interference would never be enough to stop the ritual of purging that they were about to begin but even the delay was welcome.

"Prince Otho, was your time spent in study with the high priestess successful?"

"What are you doing to him?" Otho asked again. He was closer when he spoke that time although I hadn't heard him cross the floor.

The act of turning my head to one side was painful with the bridling device on and quite useless. My eyes wouldn't see him anyway. Still, the movement was reflexive.

"You should not have come in here, Prince. There should be no witnesses to his purging. And there should most certainly not be any interference with it."

"Purging? How?"

Queen Cholla's sigh was long and heavy with impatience. I hoped she would answer Otho's question. It was one I had wished to ask ever since she first mentioned the purging. One I wished my mother had demanded the answer to, even if I understood that she had no power to stop it.

"With fire."

I jerked once more against my chains as those two words rattled through me. The sound of the chains clanking was especially loud in the silence that followed her words.

"With dragon's fire, Prince Otho. It has a peculiar quality, did you know? Your father did. It fascinated him."

There was a pause, a hiss and sizzle, and then there was a red-hot agony on the skin of my forearm. It was only in one small spot, and it was gone after only a few seconds, but it had been enough to make me buck against my bonds.

"See? There is no mark left behind. No burn. My ancestors learned long ago that those who carry the taints of the Outlands inside them are impervious to the effects of dragon fire. At first, at least. My ancestors also discovered that the dragon fire wasn't harmless to them, only that it chose to devour the taint before the flesh."

"How fascinating." Otho sounded anything but fascinated. "So, your plan is to set him on fire and let it burn until it starts to actually cause him harm?"

A series of short, sharp howls drifted into the room before Queen Cholla could answer. I didn't want to hear her answer anymore. What I wanted to do was be ill. As the knowledge of what she planned became clear, my stomach twisted in a familiar, wrenching way that had me swallowing frantically. I couldn't be sick then, not with my mouth sealed shut. But dread made me nauseous.

I waited, my body rigid and tense, but the only thing I heard was the not-so-distant howls of the Outlanders and the renewed chanting of the high priest and priestess. Pain trotted its way from my feet all the way up into my head, lingering in the very center of my head. I was so caught up in waiting for the inevitable burning that I forgot for a moment just what that pain meant.

It was the waiting I hated most, I thought.

The chant was low and incredibly fast, the strange words spilling from their lips at a rate I didn't think possible. And all that while I just waited, blind, mute, and immobile.

Waiting was the hardest part as my mind raced through the possibilities. It skipped ahead to a time when the purging had worked and I was left, broken and only half of my former self. It went to a future when the purging had failed, and I was left to the mercy of Queen Cholla. Both held their own amount of wretchedness, but I did wish I'd been allowed to choose. And both had first to face the fire. There was no avoiding that, no other option laid out to me.

I was so lost in waiting and fantasizing about my end that when the fire came rushing over me, I wasn't ready.

How could anyone be ready for that? How does one prepare oneself to be burned alive? I surely did not know.

But I hadn't done it, whatever it was.

With a whoosh that reminded me of Dragon's Nest going up in flames, my body was transported to a level of agony that it had never achieved before.

There is pain and then there is pain. The second sort cannot be put into words because, how do you describe the anguish of feeling flesh melt from bones? How do you describe heat raging through your body, making your blood boil inside your veins?

I lost hold of my own body then, my mind carried far, far away from the consuming fire. I could not honestly say if I writhed within my bonds on that table or if I'd gone completely rigid and unmoving at the intensity of the pain. I couldn't say if I made any noise past the iron bit in my mouth or if all my voice was bottled up inside me. I couldn't say if the priest and priestess continued their mindless chant or if Otho and Queen Cholla continued their cut off conversation.

There were no voices, no words, no actions inside my consciousness outside of the fire and what it was doing to my body.

And then the ferocity of that pain receded as my mind truly left the present and was swept into the future. A vision that I should have known was coming but was too anxious to give any thought to at that time.

Set against the distant backdrop of fire covering me, I saw the ivory walled city of Ludys. I saw the mountain, but it was not burning. Not yet. Smoke was billowing out of the top of it. Thick, black, noxious smoke that stained the sky and blotted out part of the sun's light, casting a long shadow on the fields before the gate of Ludys. Those fields, usually so empty in my world ending visions, were dotted with moving shapes. People, thousands of them, scurrying about like little black and brown ants.

There was a divide between the people in the fields. Those that resembled black ants were gathered to one side, facing Ludys. There were banners standing above their heads, black banners with some crimson emblem emblazoned on them. The wind caught the banners and made them snap and dance. On the other side, just outside Ludys' gates, were those who were dressed in shades of brown. Their own banners were white and gold, the symbol too pale to be made out.

Without being told I knew that they were armies. And I knew that they were gathered to make war. My vision took me closer until the people began to look less like insects and more like people, until their faces began to take shape and become recognizable. There was a familiar face in the ranks of the army of Ludys, a face whose presence I did not understand.

It was Jarris.

Except, he was different. There was something almost lifeless about his face. His eyes were glazed over as if he saw nothing in front of him. The viper-like tension that usually hummed through his body before a fight was gone, leaving him looking weak and unprepared as Queen Cholla's Purge began their charge.

I wished I had a voice in my vision to yell at him but all I could do was watch, a passive bystander to the events of the future, as the front line of Queen Cholla's Purge reached the ranks of the army of Ludys.

Jarris never even lifted a weapon. He simply stood, as did every other man with him, as they were mercilessly cut down. Their victory so swift and easy, the men of

Queen Cholla's Purge let out a collective shout of triumph.

And then it happened.

The fire the mountain had been teasing with its plume of black came forth, a fountain of flame and ash, rivers of molten rock. The fire rolled down the mountainside like a waterfall of orange.

"Free me," came the words I'd heard before. A hoarse whisper that had barely enough strength to be heard in my vision.

"Free me," it said again as the world burned and ended.

I wanted to answer that voice, to ask it who it was and what it must be freed from. But my mouth was as sealed shut in the future as it was in the present.

"Free me," it said one last time, as the future wavered and turned to dust before my eyes, returning me to the inferno of dragon's fire that awaited me in the present.

~ ~ ~

Gray shadows clung to my sight, dim outlines of people moving about in haste. Light and darkness were separated, giving some distorted sense of vision to my eyes. The blank grayness that had covered them before was lifting, lightening to more of a haze and less of a thick curtain.

If I could have roused myself further, I would have been thrilled at the development. As it was, all I could do was lie limp and imprisoned within my own body again. No muscle moved at my command. I was returned once more to the state I'd been in when Queen Cholla's men first took me.

The fire was gone.

The burning had stopped.

In its place was a numbing cold that left me shivering with tremors. Twinges of phantom pain raced through my insides.

My clothes were gone with it, apparently not as impervious to dragon's fire as my flesh was. A blanket was settled loosely over me, covering most of my body. Whoever had tossed it on me had not been at all careful about it, though, and my feet and lower legs were still bare and exposed. The cloth itched against my skin, and I longed to shift the blanket enough to cover myself fully, but my hands and arms weren't working at all.

Around me voices spoke, loud and rushed, one voice interrupting another time and again. Lying motionless and forgotten, I bent all of my focus onto following those voices.

"You will move to secure Abirell at once, Captain. That was not a suggestion on my part but an order."

"Your Majesty, I am begging you to reconsider that order. We've lost almost a quarter of our men already and more Outlanders arrive every night. There's enough of them out there now that they've made their own shadow land. Sending half the army to Abirell will almost guarantee success for the Outlanders."

"If King Mitkas of Ludys can afford to send men to Dragon's Nest, then we must be able to afford to send men to Abirell. I'm not letting him get a hold of another gateway."

"And how do you propose we defend ourselves here? We've already stripped the border guard and brought most of them here and it is still not enough. Perhaps if you'd actually used those trackers instead of banishing them, we might have made some progress."

Queen Cholla's soft footfalls went back and forth, back and forth as she paced the room.

"You forget your place, Captain. To suggest that we insult Chance by using the tainted reveals a great lapse in your own faith."

"Forgive me, Your Majesty. They were thoughtless words."

"Or not so thoughtless. You speak your mind and if that is what is in it, then we must rid you of those thoughts. Chance will see us through these times as she has always done. When you have sent the troop to Abirell, I want you to lead a raid against this shadowland you say they have created. Prove your faith to me in battle, not in useless apologies."

"As you command, Your Majesty," the captain said, his voice heavy with resignation.

I lay and listened to the sound of his retreating steps, certain that they would never return to that hall.

Queen Cholla's pacing did not end with her captain's exit. If anything, it sped up. As time inched slowly by, I wondered if she meant to pace the entire day away. And then other thoughts filled my mind. I wondered if the purging had worked and if the vision I'd had during it was the last I'd ever had. I wondered if it didn't work and if some new punishment awaited me because of my failure to be purged.

I'd made myself a promise when I ran from Dragon's Nest that I would never walk time again. I'd broken it once before out of curiosity.

As I lay there, listening to Queen Cholla pace, I decided to break it once more. Not so much out of curiosity, although I was curious about how much the queen's word was worth, but out of defiance. She'd tried to purge me of my gift, and I wanted to prove that it was still mine.

It was Mother's thread of time that I found. The last memory I had of seeing her face, although the memory was an unpleasant one. It was in those last moments before I'd yelled for those men in the courtyard to stop and stopped time itself by accident. Mother's face had been blanched and her eyes wide as she watched Ahashi being wrenched from her arms and dragged toward the center of the yard.

I followed her time all the way until Queen Cholla had her and Ahashi escorted out of the hall of Chance, promising to provide her with a room to stay in and to inform her as soon as they knew if the purging was successful.

Queen Cholla had kept her word. Mother and Ahashi were brought into a room. It was a small room, but it had an actual bed in it and a window with plain brown curtains framing it.

I watched as Mother sank onto the bed, holding Ahashi tight. I watched and I watched as the hours passed. She started from time to time, as if she heard footsteps coming down the hallway and past the door. Each time, though, she sank back in disappointment. That disappointment deepened with every passing hour; her face drawn into a tighter frown.

Someone entered the room but only to deliver food. Mother didn't touch the stuff, but Ahashi did, eating with relish. She needed the food. In just a few days, her cheeks had sunken in and taken on a sallow color. As I walked Mother's time and watched Ahashi, I knew that Mother could have done no more to save me than what she had done. She'd had Ahashi to care for still and to protect.

That didn't make it any easier to accept but at least it took the edge off my bitter disappointment.

When I left Mother's thread behind and returned to the present, Queen Cholla was still pacing. She was no longer alone, though. The gray voice of her high priest filled the room with its monotonous sound.

"The survivors of Underling Sithe's tower have been counted."

"How great were our losses?"

"Less than half have survived. Underling Sithe wishes to know what steps the crown is taking to protect his tower dwellers from further decimation."

"Underling Sithe should know better than to question his queen."

"It is not you he questions."

"Oh?" Queen Cholla paused in her pacing. Without turning my head, her gray outline was just visible to the side of me. The lines of the outline were a little sharper, the grays a little more defined.

"It is his faith he is questioning. They all do. Our faith in Chance has long been less than fervent and Chance punishes us for it."

"And what do you suggest I do?" Queen Cholla's voice rose a little higher with the question.

"It is not my place to..."

"It is your place. It is what you are forever doing. You are closer to Chance than any of us will ever be. What must we do to restore our faith in her?"

"Sacrifice."

The single word sounded so sinister on the empty voice of the high priest. It turned my blood cold.

"Sacrifice what?"

S. T. Hobbs

"You pitied the mother of that creature and have harbored it longer than you should have. Underling Sithe's tower fell last night when you allowed it to stay under your roof. Deliver it and all it carried on it and the one bonded to it back to the Outlands from whence it came. Pacify the Outlands by returning what is theirs in good condition and pacify Chance by removing the taint."

For a moment, I forgot that I was the one they were talking about. I wasn't human to them. When I remembered, everything inside of me crumpled at the high priest's suggestion.

"We must rid ourselves of every taint. Only then can we hope to triumph against the forces of the Outlands and only then can we defend against the growing power of Mitkas in Ludys."

Queen Cholla resumed her pacing. Her steps quickened. Back and forth, back and forth, the sound of her skirt swishing as gently as grass in a breeze.

"Very well, Priest. It shall be as you say. We shall return all that is tainted to the Outlands and then Chance will guide and protect us."

Chapter 29

"Y OU KNOW HOW THIS GOES, then," Keis said. "Not a sound from you or it's your tongue I take." Sitting up with my back against a wall, I managed a small nod. His words were hollow; useless threats in comparison to what I'd heard Queen Cholla agree to do with me. Every thought of mine was turned toward her final words, toward the sentence she had passed on me. Given back to the Outlands.

Except, that I'd never come from the Outlands.

A slight twist of a key, and Keis had set my mouth free once more.

His face was blurry before my eyes but at least I was beginning to see colors and more detail than just faint outlines. I could make out where the tray of food and water sat on the floor next to me and could reach a hand out to pick up the cup without groping for it.

The metal bit had been in my mouth for so long that it flavored everything my tongue touched. The water, the softened bread, the broth - it all tasted like iron. I swallowed it down despite the gagging flavor and despite my swollen tongue and raw throat.

Keis tossed a bundle towards me, and it struck me in the chest. I lifted it up, trying to make sense of it through my blurred vision.

"Why we're bothering to feed and dress you, I don't know, since you're nought but Outlander meat now. But it's Her Majesty's orders so put them on."

I suppose Queen Cholla thought it a kindness to not send me naked into the Outlands.

It took a good deal of fumbling, my hands shaking uncontrollably as the moment for my banishment drew ever nearer, but I managed to pull the clothes on.

There was a sleeveless leather jerkin similar to what I'd worn in the plains, except that the inside was lined with soft, fine fur. The pants were made out of some animal hide, softened to wear comfortably. Keis waited until I was fully dressed before tossing a pair of boots to me as well.

My fingers refused to hold still enough to tie the laces. They trembled and dropped the laces several times before Keis lost patience and did the job himself.

"I'd be all atremble myself if I knew I was going to the Outlands," he said, quite genially.

I was tempted to shove him hard for his friendliness. Why bother with it when you were just going to send someone to their death?

He shoved the metal bit back into my sore mouth before I had a chance to pull away, not at all careful of how it caught my tongue, and closed the cage once more around my head.

"Now then, let's get on with this. Her Majesty wants you turned loose out there before the sun fully sets and we've a long way down to go."

I had not tried to stand or walk since that night in the courtyard when I'd stopped time and come close to cursing the other plains people. I hadn't had the strength or the will to.

Keis made me try now.

He lifted me up off the ground and set me on my feet. My legs were as full of tremors as my hands and arms were. I wanted to crumple up into a pile again and refuse to take a single step. I wanted to fight and drag us away from our destination. It was what Jarris would have done. But I wasn't Jarris, and I did not have his strength, especially not after the vision and the purging. When Keis put his hand on my arm and shoved me forward, I complied instead of resisted.

There were stairs and more stairs. So many stairs that I decided the hall of Chance must have been the uppermost room of the tower. Winding stairs that circled around over and over again, making me dizzy.

With every passing moment my eyesight gained strength until the colors I saw were not muted and the shapes and lines I saw were not blurred. We were still climbing down the spiraling stairs when my vision cleared fully, and my sight was restored as before. Even faced with the certain knowledge that I was about to become food for the savage beasts of the Outlands, I rejoiced at the return of that sense.

Each step down brought me closer to my doom and yet I could not find it within myself to resist. Keis paused for breath on a landing, and I sank against the nearest wall, leaning against its support because I was too feeble and dizzy.

"Come on. Sun's setting soon and we've got a ways to go still," he said, a bit breathless from our climb down.

With that, Keis dragged me on again. Down even more stairs, passed cracked open doors that only half concealed the faces that peered out from behind them. I could hear some of the whispers spoken behind those half-shut doors - whispers about myself and whispers about the Outlanders and whispers about how I was one of the Outlanders and whispers about it all being my fault.

Those whispers were the hardest to hear. Their speakers would never know the full truth. I had thought we'd stopped the Outlanders' attacks on the plains people. Instead, I was pretty sure we just opened a gateway to let them in.

When we reached the end of the stairs, we were below ground in yet another tunnel that connected the thirty or so towers.

The smell of rock and damp earth and wet iron made the air inside the tunnel heavy. There was a chill in that air, too, that didn't match the bright sunshine that I'd seen glimpses of through windows as we passed them by, but I wasn't sure if it was the coolness of the air or my own terror that sent shivers down my back and through my limbs. Those shivers made each step harder to take.

How long we walked down one long tunnel after another, I don't know. I lost count of the number of times we turned down a new one. The air grew more oppressive the further we went.

I wanted to stop and rest again but Keis became more anxious the further we went, and he hurried me forward even as my feet shuffled reluctantly on.

We turned yet another corner and entered an underground room. A glance around the place showed that it was used by Queen Cholla's army. Weapons and armor hung along the walls on racks. In the center of the room, a cloaked and hooded man waited for us by a brazier of fire.

The man shifted, stirring the fire, and his hood slipped back a little revealing his scarred face and I recoiled as I recognized him as the assassin from my vision. Keis led me straight to the brazier and with a shove sent me to my

S. T. Hobbs

knees. I caught myself with my hands, the heat from the flames tightening the skin on my face.

"You're late," the scarred man said.

"Let's just get on with this," Keis said, positioning himself behind me. "We don't have much time before the sun sets."

As he spoke, Keis pulled my arms behind my back and tied them there. I was too numb with dread to fight him when he took hold of the cage that held my mouth shut and forced my head to remain in place. I knelt there, docile and compliant, as the scarred man removed a branding iron from the fire.

It wasn't until the first breath of heat brushed against the skin of my forehead that I tried to pull away but by then it was too late. Keis had firm hold of my head and the scarred man had a firm hold of his branding iron as he pushed it against my forehead.

The gifteds' resistance to dragon fire didn't carry over to ordinary fire or metal heated by ordinary fire. When the branding iron touched my forehead, it burned. It sizzled against my skin and no struggle on my part could separate me from the iron. Tears stung my eyes and then ran freely down my cheeks, stinging the raw wounds my fingernails had clawed into my skin hours before, as the iron burned deeper. My body shook with the searing pain.

When at last it was pulled away, I fell forward, barely missing the burning brazier. A sound escaped my sealed lips that didn't sound human. A whimper that sounded like a wounded animal.

I was barely aware of Keis untying my hands. I was barely aware of his hands under my arms, hauling me upward. Even the pain of the branding receded as I understood just how close I was to being thrown out on my own into the Outlands.

The numbness from before had morphed into something cold, freezing everything inside of me and leaving me on the verge of shattering into a million pieces.

Keis gave me a nudge toward the far side of the room, the gentleness of the gesture belying the severity of what he was doing to me. He pressed a sack into one of my hands, his own fingers forcing mine closed around it.

"Here's everything we took from you," Keis said.

I held it without even feeling it there. Its weight in my hand wasn't enough to penetrate the fog of disbelieving horror that settled over me as I stared at the shut door that I knew separated me from the one place I never imagined being in.

The scar faced assassin stood, one hand resting on an iron bar holding the door shut. I stared at him, at his eyes, as I approached. His eyes were cold and vacant of any emotion as he returned my gaze. There was none of the awe or the scheming or the fear in his face that others had when they looked at me. I was nothing to him. And it was nothing for him to consign me to the darkness of

S. T. Hobbs

monsters. I wondered how many others he had so callously sent to such a dark fate from that dark, lonely room.

"By order of Her Majesty, Queen Cholla of the Iron Towers, you are hereby banished to the Outlands from whence your kind came, never to return to the land of men."

His voice was as careless of my fate as his expression was. His hand moved, lifting the latch while from behind I felt Keis' hands working at the lock at the back of my head.

The door opened, revealing the swirling dark shadows, and letting in a wisp of cold, wet air. The bridling device slid off of me and a shove, far harder than the other Keis had given me before, propelled me through that open door before I could register that my mouth was free. It was hard enough to throw me on my hands and knees and the sack I'd been given slipped free and fell on its own onto the ground. My fingers dug into damp, slimy soil.

A slam told me the door was shut once more, locking me out.

I was in the Outlands.

Alone.

Alone. Alone. Alone. The word took up a rhythm inside my head, one that raced along hard enough to match the rhythm of my heart.

I didn't move from my hands and knees. I just stared and stared out into that darkness that no sight could penetrate. I just listened as the unearthly howls and snarls and calls of the Outland creatures filled the damp, cool air around me. I just breathed in the decaying scent of death that hung like a vapor in the air. And I tried to tell myself it was all just a dreadful dream.

I was in the Outlands, a place no one dared venture into and from which no one returned.

I sat there and sat there, no sense of time passing. I sat there, feeling as if I could sit there forever. And as I sat there, a strange thing happened.

I heard a song coming from the shadows. A song so low and haunting and beautiful that it took hold of the wild thumping of my heart and slowed it. It wrapped its melodious notes around my numb and frozen mind and brought it back to life. It beckoned me to come and meet it in the darkness and I left my hands and knees and found my feet, picking up the sack that had been thrust upon me. It compelled me forward with a sweetness that clashed with every scent and sight and taste of the Outlands.

That song, wordless and yet saying much, called me forward and I went.

Chapter 30

*U*NCLE MITKAS HAS OPENED *the fighting pits again that Father closed. He says that the people need some diversion from the troubles that plague us. He insisted that I come with him today on their opening day. I thought I knew what to expect since Father and Mother both told me about them. But it turns out that Uncle Mitkas had a different idea other than pitting criminals against each other in the pits.*

I'd wondered why he wanted Outlanders captured instead of killed. I found out today. He put one of the beasts in the pit with a handful of the condemned. I've never seen such a horrible sight. I asked him why he'd done it.

"Because, Rensi," he said, "our people are terrified. I want to show them that these things can be beaten. If it costs us a few thieves and murders to show that, then it's worth it to me."

I'm not sure that today's spectacle alleviated anyone's fears, though. The Outlander destroyed the men and had to be killed by soldiers in the end. I suppose watching the soldiers kill it might have done some good. To be honest, the sight of the creature made me ill even without the added horror of watching it at work. It reminded me too much of the army of Outlanders Brym held in that cavern.

Uncle Mitkas has grown more and more withdrawn as bad news arrives almost daily. We learned yesterday that Abirell was attacked by plague and that there were few survivors. News such as that sends Uncle Mitkas into a foul, silent mood where it is best to avoid him for as long as possible. He locks himself away with an ancient pile of books that he claims he found in the library but that I have never seen before. When he does come out, his eyes are always shot through with red as if he has spent many hours without blinking. I puzzle over what it is he is reading and what purpose it serves. He seems determined to find something, but I can't imagine what.

Other titles by S. T. Hobbs

The Divalian Chronicles –

Prequel ~ The Thief and the Slave

Book 1 ~ The Traitor's Alliance

Book 2 ~ The Last Chief

Book 3 ~ The Courier's Apprentice

Book 4 ~ The King's Successor

The Oracle's Odyssey –

Book 1 ~ The Forgotten Curse